THE TIME TRAVELS
of
ANNIE SESSTRY

Book One: Sly as a Fox

BRENDA WELBURN

For
Riley, Devin, and Leo

Know your history and pass it on to future generations.

Contents

Introduction

S *ly as a Fox* is the first in a trilogy on the McElmurry-Calhoun Family. *The Time Travels of Annie Sesstry* is a work of fiction; however, several characters substantiate real people. Some in this book are notable African Americans in and around Crawford County, Georgia, in 1867. Others are deceased members of the McElmurry family. Annie, Emma, and Josh are a composite of the author's grandchildren and younger, extended McElmurry-Calhoun family members. Readers will become acquainted with other descendants in the subsequent books.

The time travel series is the story of the author's family and the continuous search for at least one unidentified ancestor brought to America from Africa against their will on a ship purposed for the enslavement of human cargo. Very little information is available about the identity of the family's earliest forbearers. That scarcity of verifiable facts on the early family members fueled the decision to use the legend of an unknown ancestor and the fantasy of time travel to narrate the origin of the McElmurry-Calhoun family history in America. This tale is how the writer imagined the life of Fox and Mary McElmurry to be after the Civil War. It relies on stories from family elders and others familiar with the story. Although the tale is mostly fiction, the accomplishments of Fox and Mary's decedents are accurate. The values passed down by Fox and Mary continue to serve the family today.

Throughout the book, the writer attempts to give voice to those who were not allowed to speak their truth when brought to this land under coercion. It is understood and accepted that this part of the family history and that of all African Americans descended from enslaved people is painful. It is not an easy story to hear or to tell. Nevertheless, the McElmurry-Calhoun descendants are filled with immeasurable pride and gratitude when considering the hardships their ancestors, both known and unknown, endured to endow them with the opportunities they enjoy today. They are the descendants of solid stock.

Census records indicate Laverne "Fox" McElmurry was born somewhere in Virginia around 1829. The time of his transport from Virginia to Georgia is unknown. Members of the family have examined public and family records in search of more detailed information on Fox. No formal records of the union between Fox McElmurry and Mary Gaines have been located. Seven of their nine children were born before the Civil War. It is assumed legal authorities did not recognize their marriage at the time of their union.

This book and its sequels focus on the author's direct ancestors, beginning with Fox and Mary. The writer leaves it to other family members to tell the stories of their lineage. The writer's linear ancestor from Fox and Mary was their daughter Missouri. Missouri married Joshua Calhoun in 1885, and Book Two, *Missouri's Memories,* will feature their story.

Joshua and Missouri had eight children. Missouri outlived Joshua and resided until her death in 1943 in the Antebellum home Joshua built and bequeathed to their youngest daughter Lila Calhoun Davis. A fire in the house in 1958 destroyed Missouri's bible. It contained birth, death, and marriage dates and other vital family information. Missouri and Joshua's eldest daughter Mamie makes an appearance in this book. More of her story surfaces in *Missouri's Memories.* Mamie Calhoun Jones was the author's grandmother.

Besides telling a family's story, there are other significant lessons the writer felt compelled to emphasize. Fox was the first member of the McElmurry/Calhoun Family to register to vote on July 23, 1867. Annie, Emma, and Josh travel to the past on that day. Voting and civic engagement is a solemn responsibility, even when it is not easy and the outcome appears preordained.

Fox may not have fully believed in the system, but he was invested in the potential of the system. He understood the vision of the nation's founders. He internalized every individual's role in promoting that potential and what it would mean to his people if the vision and goals set out at the beginning of this nation could be achieved and applied to all people. Democracy and freedom are hard-fought gains and must be protected and continuously revitalized.

Finally, the foundation of this book is built on a personal belief that family is essential. History matters and the convergence of family and history is a powerful tool in understanding who and why we are. One must go or look back and understand where they came from to move forward toward who and what they want to be.

Sankofa!

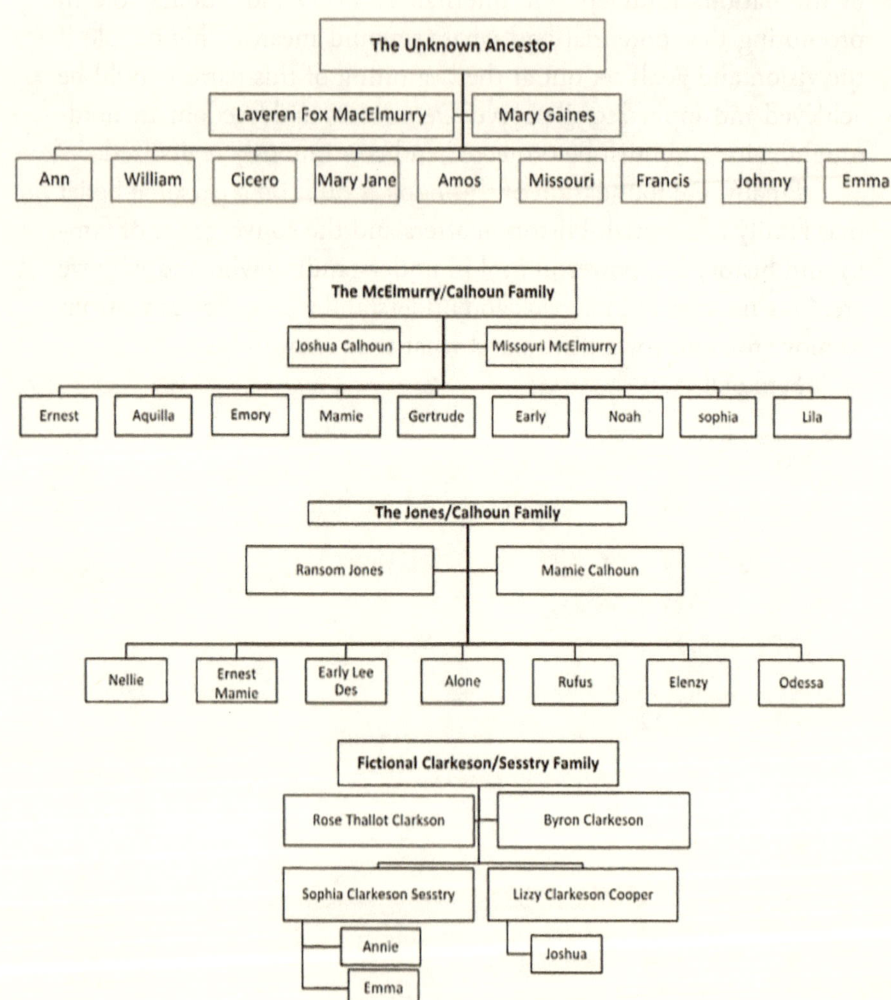

The Unknown Ancestor
Laveren Fox MacElmurry
Mary Gaines
Ann
William
Cicero
Mary Jane
Amos
Missouri
Francis
Johnny
Emma
The McElmurry/Calhoun Family
Joshua Calhoun
Missouri McElmurry
Ernest
Aquilla
Emory
Mamie
Gertrude
Early
Noah
sophia
Lila
The Jones/Calhoun Family
Ransom Jones
Mamie Calhoun
Nellie
Ernest Mamie
Early Lee Des
Alone
Rufus
Elenzy
Odessa
Fictional Clarkeson/Sesstry Family
Rose Thallot Clarkson
Byron Clarkeson
Sophia Clarkeson Sesstry
Lizzy Clarkeson Cooper
Annie
Joshua
Emma

The transatlantic slave trade began in the mid-fifteenth century. The early slave trade was dominated by Portuguese merchants who transported between ten and twelve million enslaved Africans across the Atlantic Ocean to the Caribbean and Atlantic Coast. The largest number of people taken from Africa to the Americas for enslavement were transported during the eighteenth century.

--Encyclopedia Britannica

Prologue

I am lost forever. I shall never again see the fertile lands of home. I will not behold the sun as it rises over the huts of my village and illuminates the plains of my homeland at the start of each new day. Gone forever is the warmth of its rays on my face as I lie in the grass. The vision of the azure-blue skies kissing the tops of trees and the swift flight of the gazelle and lion sprinting across the open fields are gone from me forevermore.

I do not rest beneath the glimmering sun or starry sky of the motherland. I lay shackled in the bowels of a slave ship, immersed in my own waste and that of those around me. Decay assaults my senses. The stench is an amalgamation of vomit, rotting flesh, and human misery. If there is a hell, then this is the core of its origin.

How did I come to be in this cruel place, victimized by men who bow to a god of greed? I was stolen in the dark of night like a treasure, then tossed to the dogs in the morning like a worthless bone. Warring tribes, hostile neighbors, loathsome men - black and white - guilty of unforgivable sins. Bought and sold with no contemplation of my true worth; for what price is there to be placed on an immortal soul.

To my captors, I was an adversary. To the slave traders, I am a commodity. Despair dwells deep, for I am aware when this ship arrives at its destination, I will be auctioned off to the highest bidder. I will be abused and made to face indignities no man or woman should suffer. I will be dishonored and used until I no longer serve their purposes.

When they are done, I will be discarded like feckless refuse, buried in an unmarked grave.

But I won't succumb and become the animal they perceive me to be. My spirit will rise and rebel. I will not permit them to declare me unworthy of humanity because of the color of my skin. I shall not allow them to judge me as insignificant. I am more than human substance. I have a spirit they cannot touch. I have worth. I matter to the people of my village, to my family, to the one I was to marry. I have value to the Creator even if it seems He or She has abandoned me. And I will matter to my descendants, those who will one day search for my name and give witness to my existence.

Those around me beg to die; I beg to live. I ask to pass on my essence. I plead to the Almighty power to let my spirit rise above and move through earthly dimensions to see beyond these shameful times to a better day. I will not lose myself in this netherworld. I will not surrender my soul.

I will endure.

Annie

"Rise and shine," echoed John Sesstry's voice throughout the house.

"Wake up and smell the roses," mimicked his thir-teen-year-old daughter Annie from under her covers.

"Wake up and smell the roses," rang out John's booming voice.

Annie rolled her eyes, sighing dramatically. "Here we go again. No such thing as a lazy summer Saturday for the Sesstry clan."

The Sesstry clan, as Annie put it, were part of the recent arrivals to Great Falls, Virginia, if fifteen years could be considered recent. A community of inconsistencies in Fairfax County, it was an upper-income suburb expanding and squeezing out a traditional Virginia rural horse hamlet, eighteen miles from Washington, DC. But Annie was uninterested in the ongoing skirmishes of zoning regulations and school boundaries happening in Great Falls and Fairfax County; she was too busy learning and testing out her new status as a teenager.

It had been just over a month since she had turned thirteen on June first, and she was not unlike most thirteen-year-old girls on the emotional roller-coaster of early adolescence. Happy one moment, tormented the next, refereeing the internal battle between child and emerging young woman: Daddy's girl one day, independent, rebellious teen seeking freedom the next.

Sitting up in the four-poster bed, Annie stretched and absently surveyed her bedroom. It began reflecting more of her taste and less of her mother's decorating preferences in the last few years.

Characteristic of an average teenager, the room exposed the inescapable march propelling Annie from childhood through her teenage years and on to adulthood. She still slept with her treasured, scruffy teddy bear Lulu, as she had since the age of ten months, but her room proclaimed her changing interests.

Posters of Larenz Tate, Corbin Bleu' and Jonathan Rhys Meyers hung above her bed. Word rocks, her latest obsession, were scattered on top of her dresser, nightstand' and desk. *Journey, hope, dream, dare* - simple words with reflective and potent meanings. A color-coded calendar hung near her door, reminding her of upcoming appointments and events and declaring her increasing control of her own time. Earbuds for her iPod, friendship bracelets, and a tack board covered with scraps of souvenirs and mementos signaled that Annie Sesstry was leaving the little girl behind.

The early morning sun illuminating the room cast a spotlight on one wall proclaiming not only Annie's transformation but her brilliance as well. It was the wall covered with charcoal outlines, watercolors, and pencil sketches. Annie had been drawing since she was three years old, and now at the age of thirteen, she was a skilled artist beyond her years. She could draw almost anything or anyone, and her instructor proclaimed her a gifted artist, a true phenom. A row of sketch pads and books filled the credenza adjoined to her desk. She never went anywhere without a sketchbook and did not return home without illustrations of her day's outings. The books were identical with Black canvas covers. What set each one apart from the other were the spines of the books. Annie artfully wrote the date of the first sketch of the book on its spine. When it was full, she added the date of the last drawing. The books were a record of the journey through her young life.

Annie absently looked around, drew her legs up, hugged her knees, thrust them out again, and then fell back on her bed.

"Why," she groaned, staring at the ceiling, "why do we have to spend every weekend going to museums and monuments or digging through old family photos and junk?"

It was a Sesstry family practice almost every weekend, with few exceptions. The excursions lasted for a few hours, to all day, or sometimes over a weekend. Occasionally, it was proclaimed a family vacation, though Annie hardly considered it such. Now and then, they did things Annie liked, but those times were rare.

Her parents thought her passion for art meant she relished going to all these old places for inspiration, but that wasn't true. She enjoyed the outings when she was younger, but she was a teenager now, and she wanted to do teenage things with her friends. Besides, her imagination gave her plenty of inspiration.

She promised herself in the fall, when school started; she was going to try out for a sport that had Saturday games. She wasn't athletic, nor was she interested in sports, but that didn't matter. Whatever she chose, it would get her out of these annoying hikes to all the museums and famous and not-so-famous places in the DMV.

The DMV was a catchall phrase for Washington, DC, and its neighboring states of Maryland and Virginia, and though it had a rich assortment of things to do, the Sesstrys had gone overboard and way beyond the local borders. Some of the places were cool, and she discovered interesting things to draw on their trips and local excursions, but there was something known as too much of a good thing, and Annie thought the Sesstry family was far beyond that point.

For as long as Annie could remember, the Sesstry family, her Aunt Lizzy Cooper, and her cousin Josh had been exploring old houses, museums, art galleries, even cemeteries to learn about US history; and that was the problem. Their outings were almost always about history and the past, rarely about current events or pop culture. Considerable time was spent discovering information about African American history and culture together with their own family heritage. And no good lesson on culture was complete without trying new foods that Annie often found unappetizing and challenging to digest.

They had been to the street festival in Rocky Mount, Virginia, George Washington's house in Mount Vernon, and every place else that had a connection to George and Martha, not to mention Frederick Douglass and Harriet Tubman. If George Washington slept there, the Sesstry family had dropped in. If the Underground Railroad had passed through, why, of course, they visited, even when there was nothing to see. There was not another living person out-side of her family that she knew who had been to the Contrabands and Freedmen Cemetery Memorial, the Caribbean summer festival in Norfolk, Virginia, and the H Street Festival. None who had eaten biltong, fufu, injera, and couscous.

The family had stood on the hallowed grounds of Gettysburg and walked through the cabins of the Manassas Battlefield. They visited Valley Forge, Pennsylvania, because, of course, George Washington slept there. Annie was not surprised when a promised trip to the Carowinds Amusement Park on the border of North and South Carolina turned out to be a trip to the Blackstock Slave Cemetery in Fort Mill, South Carolina, with a side trip to the park. Most of the graves at Blackstock weren't even marked, so they pro-vided little if any information about anyone.

Annie may not have grasped the point of all the trips, but she knew the cause. Annie's dad John was a curator at the Smithsonian Institution and a professor at Howard University. History was his passion, both as a profession and a hobby. That meant the rest of them, her sister Emma, her cousin Josh, her mom, and Aunt Lizzy, always had to take these strolls with him down memory lane under the guise of family outings. She had lost all interest in this stuff. Josh liked the excursions, and Emma always found ways to entertain herself regardless of where she was; but she, Ann Sophia Sesstry, had had enough, and she could find better things to do on a Saturday morning than traipse through the dusty old past.

Annie earned no sympathy from her mother Sophia for her irri-tation with visits around the city and beyond. Sophie, as she was called by most people, was a writer and returned home motivated and exhilarated about burgeoning projects inspired by their adven-tures. Like her husband, she was a history enthusiast. Her books on African American characters were inspired by her ancestors' stories and the family stories shared by friends and sometimes by strangers. Her website invited people to share their family history and stories, and Sophie could weave a tale from even the tiniest bit of informa-tion. She said the places they visited gave her context for the location of her stories. John was a historian by profession, but Sophie's love of history was by calling, and her obsession matched and frequently exceeded John's when it came to genealogical research.

When they weren't visiting places like Mary McCleod Bethune's Council House or Thomas Jefferson's Monticello, Sophie had her clan combing census records and other registers to learn more about where they came from, who their ancestors were, and to provide research for her books. The stories were an expression of Sophie's devotion to her family history and the tales passed down through the generations. She often said they were a gift and a tribute to the ancestors who came before them, especially the ones whose identity had been lost because of slavery.

Annie had studied the 'theory of context' in art class and understood its application, but she was indifferent about the past. Old stories didn't interest or concern her, and she would never paint or draw pictures of the past. She would paint the here and now, or better yet, she would paint the future as she imagined it would be. What use was there in fixating on the past?

Annie was yanked back from her reverie to the present when her ten-year-old sister Emma bounced into her room, fully dressed, perky, and with her constant cheery smile and sense of urgency. As usual, her curly hair was wild and crazy, though Emma never seemed to care. Annie thought her outfit was something Katy Perry would wear - rainbow capris leggings, a tee-shirt with a giant swirl lollypop in the center, pink socks, dangling turquoise earrings, and turquoise high-top sneakers.

The two girls were an amalgamation of their parents and looked strikingly similar. They had long legs, curly hair, and beautiful caramel-colored skin. The curls, both hers and Emma's, were compliments of their father, who had a giant curly Afro. Annie made every effort to tame her long, frizzy locks, Emma embraced them. Annie was convinced she did things to make them more unruly if that were possible. Their almond-shaped eyes with perfectly curved eyebrows were the envy of every girl Annie knew.

But the similarities ended with their physical appearance. Annie was reserved and introspective, and her energy went into her art. Her choice of clothing was simple and classic. Emma was a walking, or more accurately, a running ball of energy invoking a smile from people by her mere presence. Annie would never wear an outfit like the one Emma wore. Emma, on the other hand, wanted Annie to put some 'life' into her style. She often asked why her sister's flair for art didn't carry over to her wardrobe.

"Let's go, Ann; Dad promised a breakfast stop if we hurry."

"Don't you ever think about anything other than your stomach?" Annie shot back. Giving her sister the once-over, she growled, "I hope you plan to do something with that hair before we go. And how many times do I have to tell you to call me Annie, not Ann."

"Sorry, *Annie*," crowed Emma as she backed out of the room.

Watching her sister leave, Annie swore when she got older, she was going to change her name to Adara or something else sophisticated.

Annie was immediately sorry for snapping at Emma. Emma was funny, loving, and carefree. As far as little sisters went, she wasn't so bad, and they got along most of the time; it was just the name thing that bothered Annie.

She rolled out of bed and wondered for the millionth time - what were her parents thinking naming her Ann with the last name Sesstry. Every teacher since preschool did a double-take when they called her name – Ann Sesstry - then gave her a sympathetic smile or masked a smirk, proving they too speculated on her parents' sanity when she was named.

Annie didn't remember when her name became the target of ancestor jokes. She possessed the self-confidence to take a joke or stand up to bullies, but the stupid comments annoyed her. In fourth grade, she began referring to herself as Annie, but her family continued to call her Ann. Her friends and her teachers called her Annie. Why couldn't her family cooperate and do the same? Was that too much to ask? Better yet, why couldn't they call her Adara. Ann had read a book in which the main character's name was Adara, and she thought it was the best name ever. As she gazed into the mirror, she posed, flicked her natural curls, and thought *I even look like an Adara.*

Annie finished dressing for the day's outing in skinny jeans, a white tee-shirt, and gold post earrings. She pulled her hair back in a curly puff and applied lip gloss which she started wearing after her thirteenth birthday. For the millionth time, Annie wished again that she had a cool contemporary name like her best friends Kristen and Cody. *No,* she thought sadly, *Emma, Josh, and I have to have pre-historic names from mom's family.* Her mom always made a point of telling Josh that there had been a Joshua in every generation of their family since her great-great-grandfather Joshua Calhoun. She would then go on to tell them for the hundredth time that Ann was named for the eldest sister of Sophie's great-great-grandmother Missouri. Missouri McElmurry Calhoun was Joshua Calhoun's wife. Emma was named for the youngest McElmurry daughter. Whenever Annie complained about her name, her mother would say, "Look on the bright side, you could have been named after a state in the Midwest."

So much ado about a name, she thought. *What did it matter?*

Annie turned and took one final look in the mirror before heading out. For a nanosecond, the image that looked back was not her own. The person in the mirror resembled her, but it was definitely not her. The hair was different, the skin tone was darker, and her clothes were dated. Annie blinked her eyes tightly and opened them to find her own image staring back at her. Her stomach did a small flutter.

"Weird," she muttered as she left her room.

Just Another Saturday

Annie skipped down the back steps and, as expected, found her cousin Joshua in the kitchen sipping orange juice. Her mother was brewing her tea. The mood of the kitchen was a lot brighter than Annie's frame of mind. Sunlight bathed the large country kitchen and stainless steel appliances, radiating a taste of the glorious summer day to come. Chatter about the scheduled activities of the weekend had already begun as the microwave beeped and the refrigerator door opened and closed. The kitchen was the heart of the Sesstry household and communicated to everyone who entered; this was a place where family gathered.

"Good morning, Ann," Joshua quipped when she entered the kitchen.

"It's Annie," she shot back rudely, heading toward the subzero refrigerator.

Instantly irritated with Annie's attitude, Sophie gave her the infamous look, the one that told her children they were treading on dangerous ground. "Joshua said good morning to you… Ann." She made her point, emphasizing her daughter's given name.

"Hey Josh," sneered Annie, catching her mother's warning tone, "all ready for today's great adventure?"

Ignoring his cousin's brusque attitude, Josh nodded vigorously. "I've been thinking and about it all week. This is a spectacular monument and, as you are aware, and according to everything I've read, a long time in the making."

"Loads can happen in seven days, Josh; it's pretty pathetic you wasted a whole week thinking about the MLK Memorial. Besides, it's not like we haven't seen it before."

"I'm warning you, Ann, not today," returned her mother's stern voice from the other side of the kitchen.

Exhaling and rolling her eyes, Annie draped her arm around Josh's shoulder and kissed him on the cheek. "Just kidding Josh, you're right, it is a special monument, and Dad wants to be sure we spend time there before the African American Museum opens in a few months, putting everything in proper perspective," she intoned with a deep voice mocking her father. "You know how it is; school never ends around here."

"Learning never ends around here," her mother rejoined. "And you will appreciate that fact one day."

Annie was not being intentionally mean to Josh. She didn't define him by his circumstances, especially his grief. Contrary to the rest of the family, she did not treat him as if he were made of glass. She made fun of Josh because he was too formal and serious for his age and because kids tease each other. Josh was a kid just like any other, only one who had lost his father. Annie loved him unconditionally, and that meant not characterizing him by the tragedy that took his father.

Darryl Cooper was a graduate of West Point and had died in Afghanistan nearly two years before. Josh's pain at his father's loss could be all-consuming if he allowed himself constantly to dwell on it. He worked hard to lose himself in school, books, family, and anything else that could take his mind away from the reality that he would never see his father again. Annie thought the family made the situation worse for Josh by walking on eggshells whenever Darryl's name came up, and she knew Josh was frustrated by the fragile treatment.

Annie fought any urge to let her sympathy get in the way of treating Josh like a normal kid, which included picking on him. Preparing for the weekly outings helped Josh to focus on what was coming, not what had been; teasing him was one of the ways Annie kept their relationship as much the same as it was before her uncle Darryl's death. As his older cousin, it was her job to be annoying.

Josh was eleven years old. Shy, skinny, and tall for his age, people remarked how he was the spitting image of his father. He wore Harry Potter glasses and lived up to the brainy image he portrayed by getting all As in school. He was an ardent reader and lost himself in books of all subject matter. He thought of reading as an adventure, and he appreciated learning new things, seeing fresh places, and meeting new people through the eyes of creative writers. With books, he could use his imagination to go from a pirate ship to a rocket ship. He solved mysteries with Detective Encyclopedia Brown and joined in the westward expansion all the way to the Oregon Trail. Taking after his Aunt Sophie, he wrote stories of his own as well.

Sophie and Josh's mother, Lizzy, were sisters and best friends. Sophie's style was Boho chic; layered clothing marked by colorful, tie-dyed skirts, or full pajama pants, and funky jewelry. A grown-up version of Emma, Lizzy teased her, calling her a child of the 60s. Lizzy, on the other hand, when she wasn't wearing hospital scrubs, was Annie's adult role model for fashion, usually going for a preppier style. Both women gave off a certain vibe and pride in who they were and passed it on to their children.

Annie and Emma were being raised with an equivalent level of confidence, and people saw them as miniature versions of Lizzy and Sophie, though a bit farther apart in age. Lizzy and Sophie were a year apart, Lizzy had spent the early years of her marriage traveling around as a military spouse, but the two women never let distance get in the way of their affection and connection with each other. That Annie and Emma were growing up much the same reflected how much they connected with Sophie and Lizzy's relationship.

When Darryl was deployed to Afghanistan for the second time, they decided it was best if Lizzy took a job closer to home. They moved to the same Great Falls neighborhood in Virginia, where Sophie and her family lived. It was close to Washington, DC, where she worked and with her husband away, being near family had its advantages. When Darryl died, it was helpful for both Lizzy and Josh to have family nearby. It was especially supportive for Josh to have Annie and Emma. They were the siblings he didn't have.

Lizzy was an obstetrician, and the rotation of her practice and the pending arrival of a new baby determined her schedule. She joined in the weekly Sesstry outings when time allowed. When it didn't, she was grateful for her sister and her family. As an only child with a mother who worked odd hours, it wasn't unusual for Josh to be at the Sesstry house as much as he was at home. The arrangement worked for everyone. John could be a father figure to Josh, and Josh gave some testosterone balance to the female-dominated Sesstry clan. He was a regular on their history jaunts, and he knew the routine. It was a bonus that Lizzy and Sophie's parents lived in Washington, DC, and friends and family were abundant throughout the DMV. The Sesstry home was the family hangout. No one hosted better parties than Sophie, especially when she had Lizzy to help. Now the two families relied on each other and appreciated the comradery their living arrangement provided.

Ignoring her daughter's eye roll, Sophie went through her usual routine, making sure they were prepared for the day.

"Everybody wearing comfortable shoes?"

"Check."

"Everyone have Metro cards and water?"

"Check," replied Emma and Josh enjoying the anticipated inventory.

"Good attitudes?" she asked, looking purposefully at Annie.

"Check and double-check," roared Emma and Josh.

"Corny," murmured Annie.

She was elated her mother's checklist made no mention of cell phones. It wouldn't have mattered much since Annie, as the oldest, was the only one with a phone. It was a gift for her birthday, but outside use of the phone was mostly restricted to when Annie was away from her parents. The phone came with so many rules and conditions, she sometimes wondered what was the point of having it. But she had coveted her friends' phones, and now she had one of her, and that was huge. Her mother hadn't mentioned it today, nor had she prohibited her from bringing it, so she had tucked it into her backpack with her sketchbook. If they found out that she had it with her, she would tell them she brought it to take pictures, not to text Kristen and Cody. Texting on family outings was taboo.

John Sesstry strolled into the kitchen. He was average build but pontificated with the deep baritone cadence of a much larger man. With glasses perched on the bridge of his nose, he surveyed his household and spoke to the gathered family members as if addressing a lecture hall of students at the university. "As you all will appreciate, today's excursion is to the Dr. Martin Luther King, Jr. Memorial. Our first trip to the monument was simply a rudimentary exploration. We stopped by on our way home from another expedition. Today, we are going to expand our understanding of Dr. King's life and his contributions in the struggle for civil rights. Tell me what you learned when you researched the monument."

Sophie and John insisted the three of them research information about their outings in advance. Sophie declared, "the things you investigate for yourselves will be the things you remember most." Hence for practically all their family field trips, they had to find at least one fact about their planned destination to share with everyone before they headed out.

Josh was the first to speak.

"The statue of Dr. King is thirty feet tall, and the official address of the monument is 1964 Independence Avenue, named for the 1964 Civil Rights Act."

"Dr. King was a member of the Alpha Phi Alpha Fraternity, just like you, Daddy," beamed Emma. "It was the fraternity that first had the idea to build a monument to Dr. King, and it took almost twenty years to raise the money and build the statue."

John smiled proudly, nodding at Emma. "The fraternity had many men who were vital to the Civil Rights Movement. Brother W. E. B. DuBois was the co-founder of the NAACP."

"*Daddy's girl,*" thought Annie.

"Dr. King's wife, Coretta Scott King, was an honorary member of Alpha Kappa Alpha, Mom and Aunt Sophie's sorority," added Josh. Sophie smiled. "Both organizations have been active in the fight for civil rights."

"Ann, what about you," her father asked, turning to her, "what did you learn about the memorial?"

Annie almost commented it was just a stupid statue to get a rise out of her parents, but she had learned not to annoy them by having snarky answers to their questions. It was even worse to ignore the assignment to conduct the research and recite a fact about what they were going to see. She learned those lessons the hard way, being grounded for three days after an impertinent comment one week and failing to complete the assignment at all during another.

Truthfully, the artist in her was fascinated with the design of the statue, and she had researched the work and the artist in detail. Master Lei Yixin was the sculptor selected to design the King statue, though not without controversy because he was not Black. Born in China, he worked all over the world. Much like her, as a youth, Master Lei kept a journal of his drawings the way she kept sketchbooks of her art. He submitted the journal as his portfolio when he applied to college, where he majored in art.

"The sculpture was done by Master Lei Yixin in his homeland, China. Individual pieces of granite were sent to China, where he created 80 percent of the memorial. It was then disassembled and sent to Washington through Baltimore, Maryland, and he came to Washington to complete the final 20 percent. The theme of the work is 'Out of the Mountain of Despair, a Stone of Hope.' It's displayed in three pieces; two of the pieces represent the sides of the Mountain of Despair, and the third piece, the statue of Dr. King, is in front of the two pieces and is made to appear as if it was carved out of the mountain and came forth. Dr. King is the Stone of Hope."

For a moment, John stared at his daughter in awe. Rarely did she utter more than a perfunctory sentence about something they were going to see, making it clear she had no interest in what they were doing regardless of what it was.

"Outstanding," said John, then spreading his arms as if enveloping them, "all three of you, outstanding."

"Daddy, I don't understand the Mountain and the Stone," said Emma.

Josh jumped in. "That line is from Dr. King's 'I Have a Dream' speech. Our ancestors were slaves Emma, and the Mountain of Despair represents slavery. Even a hundred years after slavery ended, Black people were still fighting for their rights. Dr. King led the Civil Rights Movement for justice and freedom, making him the Symbol of Hope."

Good job, Josh," acknowledged Sophie, "but you shouldn't refer to our ancestors as slaves. They were enslaved people. Calling them slaves diminishes their dignity as people." The period of slavery was the most vile and evil period in American history. Our ancestors shouldn't be forced to carry the label forced on them by their enslavers."

John interrupted. "As a historian, I take some issue with your distinction Sophie. I am familiar with the movement among writers and some historians as well to eliminate the use of the word *slave* all together, but Africans and Americans of African descent who were enslaved were called slaves and even self-identified as slaves. At the museum, our references are to enslaved people. However, the use of the word slave in its historical context is correct. When we try to teach a lesson by changing a word here and ignoring the historical context there to satisfy one group or another, something is lost in the telling of the story. In *the Slave Narratives of 1936 Through 38* Federal Writers' Project, that is how former slaves self-identified."

"Yes, but…"

"All right," interjected Annie, accustomed to her parents' discussions on semantics, mostly, the creative writer versus the historian. "Are we going or not?"

"There's a lot more to the memorial than the statue," said John as he picked up his backpack. "There is symbolism in its location and its proximity to the Lincoln Memorial steps where Dr. King delivered the 'I Have a Dream' speech," and there is a wall with many quotes from Dr. King and quotes on all three pieces of the mountain." Gazing at the barely tolerant expression on everyone's faces, John announced, "and now it's time to get going if we want to stop for breakfast."

They headed toward the door leading to the garage, and Sophie glanced back at her daughter.

"Ann, why don't you bring your phone. Who knows, you might want to take some pictures." As Annie stared at her mother, Sophie shook her head and laughed. "When are you kids going to realize that I perceive it before you think it?"

<hr>

John pulled the oversized, white Chevy Suburban onto Walker Road and drove past Great Falls Village. Walker Road divided the two primary shopping areas of the village, which included a supermarket and several other small shopping venues. There had been resistance from long-time residents of the community to make changes to the village area for fear of excessive development.

The new post office and fire station were the exceptions to the effort to keep the village as it had been for many years. As a rule, most people drove to the village for basics but traveled to the more abundant malls and shopping centers for more diverse shopping. For that reason, it was odd when Annie glanced up from her phone in time to catch a glimpse of an African American teenage girl standing on the side of the road dressed in an outfit from the early twentieth century. The girl was gazinging at Annie. Annie turned to Emma and said, "Look at that girl."

"What girl?" asked Emma.

"That girl." Annie turned around again, but there was no sign of the teenager. She strained her neck to see if she could spot her, but there was no trace.

How bizarre, thought Annie. The girl's clothing was odd for the warm weather and odd for current times. *What was a Black girl in old-fashioned clothes doing standing on the side of the road in Great Falls? How could she move from sight so quickly?*

Maybe there's going to be a re-enactment event on the greens by the bandstand, she mused. *It's almost the Fourth, and they have events there all the time. But why wouldn't Dad choose that for today's activity with it being so close to home and probably something about this area? He's on the Great Falls Community Board and familiar with all the events and activities in the village, so he would have to be aware of the enactment.*

Annie twisted around one last time as they turned on to Georgetown Pike, thinking what an odd morning it had been. First, there was the aberration in the mirror and now this girl near the village. Who was she, Annie wondered, and why was she observing me?

Arrival

I am one of the strong. Strong of body, strong of mind, for my survival depends on it. Still, I am sure the body and spirit were not created to absorb assault such as this. Daily, life seeps from the crush of bodies that lie in the darkness below. But I endure. We are brought into the light for exercise, to dance and hop like fools for the amusement of soulless men. They suppose this occasional imprudent movement will minimize the disintegration of our bodies. But the conditions of the burrow, the meager rations, and the abuse ravaged on each of us is too much for many on this baleful voyage.

Some have passed violently, convulsing and choking on their own spit. More slipped away in their sleep without notice. Others with strength and speed found eternal freedom, bolting from their captors and casting themselves into the depths of the ocean. They would rather drown and rest on the bottom of the sea than accept the outcome of this crossing. I choose to live. My story will not end with this journey. It won't end with the last breath of life in a distant land. When the final chapter of my story and the story of millions more like me is written, we will be triumphant, and the captors will be confounded to understand the race of men they created, men and women who, despite all odds, survived.

There is no way to tell how long we have been on this vessel. In their subjacent dungeon, it is difficult to distinguish night from day. There is no pattern to the days when each has a turn to perform for the privilege of being mocked and the reward of taking in the fresh salt air and seeing the light of day. There is no way to count the majestic ascensions of the sun *or the risings of the full moon. These are the ways I was taught to mark time, but I have been robbed of these tools.*

But now the routine has changed. Some, such as I, have been brought on to the upper deck this night. I raise my eyes and see the waxing crescent of a new moon. The smell of the air is different. I am certain we are nearing the end of our sojourn. I am obliged to wash and scrub the deck. My spirit struggles to tell them there is no washing away their vile sins. For a moment, I see a dark shadow cross their faces, and I sense their spirits have heard.

As night gives way to dawn, I catch a glimpse of land. The lookout sees it as well, for a gun is fired, declaring our pending arrival. Three blasts announcing the most recent souls, stolen from their homeland, here to make light their simple burdens of caring for their fields and their children. The shipped is readied. My compatriots are forced to carry our dead and dying infirmed brothers and sisters above board and to toss them into the sea with the muck and sewage.

The ship will remain in port for several days to ensure we do not bring disease to this fragile people. I view them and think, yes, you are fragile slaver, and because of that, you will feel the wrath of the Creator.

The Code We Live By

Annie didn't consider her mother a helicopter parent, but the importance of family first was frequently impressed upon her and Emma. It was a value she knew had been passed on from one generation to the next. Never forget family. Never take your family for granted. It was the code her mother grew up with and the orthodoxy that ruled the Sesstry household. It was drilled into them that family was at the core of all that mattered. The code extended beyond the immediate family. If there was a choice between a family activity or outing and something else, the family won out. If there was an event at school, a dance recital, or piano concert, no kid had a greater fan base than one of the Sesstry kids or Joshua Cooper. The same was true for the multitude of extended cousins throughout the DMV. They went to things in droves.

Annie routinely heard her grandmother Rose, called Gramby by her grandchildren, chant, "God first, family second, everything else falls into place after that." Annie knew her mother had learned the lesson well. The Clarkson family cherished traditions, and Sophie combined those traditions she had practiced growing up into her own family practices. She created new customs for her family unit that felt right to her for the times and for her Annie and Emma, but she never forgot the past, never neglected family traditions.

Family meals were an abiding practice during Sophie and Lizzy's childhood. Their mother insisted the family have breakfast and dinner together. Absences and excuses were rarely tolerated. Rose would delay the start of an evening meal until everyone was seated at the table. "Meals bring a family together," Rose Clarkson announced, and no one challenged Rose Clarkson in her house.

Sophie preserved a modified version of the routine when her children, as soon as they were old enough to sit in a highchair. She was grateful John accepted and embraced her commitment to the practice and never made fun of how fastidious she was about it. They had dinner together in the evening when it was possible, and always on Sundays. The flexibility of Sophie's career and schedule meant she had breakfast and dinner with Annie and Emma practically every day, even with the demands of dance lessons, art instruction, soccer practice, and the assortment of other things the girls were involved in. Her friends considered the devotion to family meals admirable, crazy in the mayhem of modern life, and all but impossible to uphold. But for Sophie, it was non-negotiable, and she found ways to make it work.

Sophie and John believed mealtimes, whether at home around their own table or in a local restaurant such as the frequented Rutledge Diner in McLean, gave them the occasion to have fun and nurture their nuclear family. Sometimes the meals were raucous game nights over pizza or culinary experiments with everyone joining in the preparation. The menu and format were immaterial; the important thing was they set aside the challenges of the day and focused on family. It was a time when John and Sophie observed Annie and Emma and gave them their undivided attention. At home or away, there were strict rules about mealtime - no television, no cell phones, no gaming devices - that went for Sophie, John, the girls, and Josh when he was around. Lizzy was the exception because, as a physician, there were times she needed to have immediate contact with patients or the hospital.

The value of conversation was never underestimated, never belittled, and always practiced. Arguments were off-limits at mealtimes, though healthy debates on divergent views were encouraged. There was always an expectation that a position would be defended with substance. The payoff for these exchanges was evident in the girls' schoolwork and in their capacity to hold their own with peers and adults, though not always appreciated by the adults.

The Sesstrys employed family powwows and meetings for serious issues and discussions. Annie and Emma could anticipate individual time and outings with their parents, including dad-and-daughter or mom-and-daughter days out. They also had a practice they called moratoriums when the girls wanted to discuss or confess something without fear of judgment or punishment. Truth and resolution were more important than punishment if a serious problem needed to be addressed or resolved. Annie and Emma never abused the moratorium and used it sparingly; John and Sophie held to their word not to punish their daughters if they came clean. Annie and Emma were being raised in the most loving and secure environment possible.

Sophie insisted she could tell if her children grew by a fraction of an inch when they sat down for breakfast. She measured each stage of their development, every milestone by the changes in their meal choices, the tone of their voices, and the looks in their eyes. She could read their moods and knew how their day had gone just by watching them at dinner. The slow, easy smile or the down-turned mouth drew Sophie's antennae and signaled when it was time for action on behalf of her daughters.

When they ate out, the family did not have meals at fast-food restaurants. They weren't opposed to fast food, at least John and the girls weren't, but Sophie believed the time they spent waiting for their food to be served created another opening to talk and share information. On-road trips, they sought out local diners and restaurants they had scrutinized online before heading out. They explored local shops filled with odd items and old-fashioned candy. John had lengthy stories about what was going on when this candy or that game was popular. They always left with something no one needed but was always good for a joke or a story. John had many stories about a great many things. Sophie seemed to relish anything that opened a window into the past.

When they ate breakfast in the surrounding area of their Great Falls home, it was usually at the Rutledge Diner. The informal atmosphere was practically like eating at a friend's house. The whiteboard advertised the day's specials, and Josh always whooped at the prospect of corned beef hash and grits. The food was homemade, and most of the patrons were local people. The diner had been in the Rutledge family for four generations, and the staff knew John, Sophie, and the kids. They were familiar with their Saturday morning or weekend outings and took an interest in their excursions.

On this temperate July morning, the Sesstry family sat in a large booth in the back of the restaurant where the five of them could fit comfortably. There was always room to squeeze Lizzy in if she stopped by.

"Where to this morning Josh," asked Ashley Rutledge as she took their drink orders.

"The Martin Luther King Jr. Memorial."

"Good one," she nodded. "Well it is a beautiful day for an adventure."

What adventure thought Annie; *it's just another Capitol City monument.* This wasn't the first time they visited the King Memorial, and with its proximity to the mall and all the other well-known monuments and museums, it wouldn't be the last. She didn't want to break it to Ashley, but not a single visit to any memorial or monument could be characterized as an adventure. Just as she had earlier that morning, she brooded over the weekly highjack of her Saturday and thought nothing could happen at the MLK Memorial that could compensate for having to spend another Saturday listening to her father drone on about some insignificant historical detail no one cared about.

Lizzy Cooper blasted into the diner, almost knocking Ashley over as she rushed to the booth holding her family.

"Hey, gang. Just thought I'd run down for coffee. I can't stay. I need to be back at the hospital for a C-section."

Annie grinned, knowing her aunt would eat the equivalent of a full meal, nibbling off everyone's plate. Dressed in hospital scrubs and sneakers, Lizzy winked at Annie as she slid in the booth and placed a sloppy kiss on Josh with the anticipated reward of an 'ewe.' She was fun and easygoing, and Annie adored her. "Aunt Lizzy gets me," she frequently told her parents. Lizzy also earned extra points because she called her Annie. *Her mom dressed like the cool one, but aunt Lizzy was the cool one.* She thought.

"If everything goes as planned, I will meet you for a late lunch and spend the rest of the day with you guys," explained Lizzy

Darn, thought Annie, *this is going to turn into another all-day event.*

Catching Annie's facial expression, Lizzy continued,

"Soph, you can make sandwiches when I get off or order a pizza. I made a peach cobbler last night; we can have that for dessert. The kids can eat and hang out or do whatever."

Annie's face brightened.

Sophie and Lizzy had been discussing Annie's burgeoning adolescence. Sophie was growing impatient with Annie's increasing snarkiness. Lizzy was aware of Annie's plan to try out for a sport to get out of the Saturday outings and thought it was the wrong reason to take up a new activity. The two of them needed an intervention, and soon, she thought.

Lizzy understood that Sophie wanted to hold on to her "baby" a while longer but thought it was time to give her niece a bit more space. She warned her sister that holding Annie too tight could fracture the relationship. She spoke from experience. It had happened between Lizzy and Rose, and a lot went into restoring their relationship. Sophie, too remembered the battles between her mother and sister. The last thing she wanted was to fight with her daughter or to drive Annie underground with secrets and furtive behavior.

The family chatted and laughed while they ate, though Annie was unusually quiet. Lizzy stayed longer than she intended. She grabbed a piece of bacon from John's plate, a spoonful of grits from Josh's, a bit of eggs from Emma, assuming she would never eat them all until Lizzy had filled a bread plate with enough food to compile breakfast just as Annie knew she would. Lizzy wasn't all that concerned about getting back to the hospital because Chain Bridge Road wouldn't be crowded at this time of morning, and she could be back at Georgetown Hospital in no time. If anything changed with her patient, the hospital would contact her

Talking all at once, they rattled on about family plans and anticipated comings and goings. They were all headed to Martha's Vineyard with Sophie and Lizzy's parents for vacation next month, and soon after their return, Josh would start middle school. John was knee-deep in the plans for the upcoming opening of the African American History and Culture Museum. Sophie had a signing event planned for a new book on 'Blacks and the Roaring Twenties' during the Congressional Black Caucus Week. Emma had moved to the next level in soccer and was going to play on the county-wide soccer team for her age group in the fall.

"What about you Annie, what's exciting in your life?"

Annie was engrossed in her thoughts about the image in the mirror of the strange girl near the village and missed the question.

"Earth to Annie," said Lizzy, what's exciting in your life?"

"Not much," shrugged Annie.

"Dance will be starting again soon," said Sophie, "and her art lessons are going very well. This is the final year of middle school, then Langley High School, here she comes. Can you believe it? High school. Time will fly, and soon she'll be off to college."

"Wow," drawled Lizzy, "And you will be moving into senior teens in Jack and Jill too. Lots of cute boys when you go to teen conference."

"Let's not rush all of this," growled John.

Rolling her eyes and ignoring her mother and aunt's banter, Annie turned her attention to her father.

"Dad, what kind of enactment is going on at the Greens today?"

"There is no enactment," said John. "Everyone is focused on getting set up for the Fourth of July."

"Are there dress rehearsals for the Fourth?"

There's no need for dress rehearsals. It's just the traditional Independence Day festivities with music, hot dogs, and fireworks."

"So, what do you think is going on with that Black girl on the side of the road dressed in the old-fashioned clothes."

"Ann, I don't know what you're talking about."

"When we passed the village, there was a Black girl around fifteen or sixteen wearing clothes that could have been a hundred years old. I can't believe you didn't see her."

"Sorry, baby, I didn't see anyone."

"It would be hard to miss a Black girl in Great Falls that we didn't recognize," said Sophie.

Annie glanced around the table. "None of you saw a girl in a long dark skirt, a white blouse, a necktie, and a straw hat?" she asked incredulously. Annie's eyes narrowed as she scanned the blank faces of her family. They stared back at her, perplexed.

"Don't look at me like that. I know what I saw," she said, crossing her arms.

Sweat trickled down Annie's neck. At the same time, she felt a chill course through her body and a knot form in her stomach. Mildly nauseous, she asked Ashley for a glass of ginger ale to settle her stomach.

There's something up with that girl, she thought, and though she couldn't explain it, she felt it had some connection to her family.

When they were done with breakfast, they gathered their things and once again piled into the car. Annie kept watching as John drove toward Reston, convinced she would see the girl again. They left the car at the Reston Station. It was pointless to drive into the District with all its traffic and parking problems. Saturdays did not bestow immunity on locals from the tourists, especially with the Fourth of July approaching. As a matter of fact, it gave locals the opportunity to take advantage of the many entertainment options the city offered, increasing the crowds even more. Her father was fond of saying the city belonged to the nation, and he loved seeing people take advantage of all the city had to offer. "Not many capital cities in the world offered so much for free" was one of his favorite sayings.

Emma contentedly patted her full stomach and gibbered about anything that came to mind. Josh reviewed the information on the monument he had picked up at the library. Annie's thoughts still focused on the peculiar girl in the village and the perplexing image in the mirror. Making their way from the parking garage to the station, a girl bumped into Annie. Annie peered at the girl. It was her! She wasn't dressed in the dated outfit, but Annie was sure it was her. The girl glimpsed at Annie perplexed for a moment, showed no sign of recognition, and continued moving.

Weird, Annie thought for the second time that morning.

They made their way to the platform with the easygoing swagger associated with familiarity and comfort with their surroundings and practice of riding the Metro. They were hometown people going about their everyday practices. Annie was getting into the spirit of the day teasing Josh and Emma, despite her earlier tween misgivings and moodiness. The wait for the train was brief, and they had their pick of seats since it was early, and the Reston Station was the origination point for the Silver Line of the Metro.

John and Sophie sat in a double seat across the aisle from the kids, observing the natural intimacy that comes from being family and spending time together. Emma was perched next to Annie, and Josh was standing, wrapped around the stanchion pole for standing passengers peering over her shoulder as she pulled out her sketchbook. With all her bluster and complaining, Annie loved and protected her younger sister and the cousin, who was more like a brother to her. They admired her, and she basked in the attention they showered on her. Savoring their excitement and anticipation when she drew comical sketches, this morning, she had a captive audience.

Sophie and John watched Annie appreciatively as she drafted something in the ever-present sketchbook to the amusement of Emma and Josh. The vibration of the train did not affect the rapid sail of her pen as she drew. Soon the three of them were laughing uncontrollably, and Sophie wished she could see what fantastic tale Annie wove with the magic of her pen. Annie could tell a story with her sketches as effortlessly as Sophie could create a story sitting at her computer.

John fixed his gaze wistfully on his eldest child. "Ah, I almost see her."

"Who?"

"The sweet little girl that was our daughter before the *Invasion of the Body Snatchers* marauded our household."

Sophie chuckled.

"Maybe," John pondered, "we should visit the *Exorcist* steps in Georgetown on the off chance we'll find a priest who wants to cast out a demon named Adara."

"Oh, first *the Invasion of the Body Snatchers*, now *the Exorcist*; I guess it's a movie theme today."

"Not a bad idea. We can watch *Selma* when we get home to cap off our day at the King Memorial."

"Don't go overboard, honey. The kids are getting older, and they like to have some of their weekends to themselves, especially Ann."

"What's wrong with spending time with family? What's that your mother always says, God first, family second, everything else after that. Besides, we did it all the time when I was growing up."

"You grew up in a macho household. Your poor mother didn't have a chance with a husband and three sons. Family activities for the five of you consisted of watching soccer, playing football, or going to Yankee Stadium."

"We had Sunday dinner together," he smirked.

"Yeah, in front of the television watching football, baseball, or any other sporting event you could find. We are well aware your father is a sports fanatic and your mother gave up trying to enculturate him to other experiences a long time ago."

"Well, you've done a fine job of enculturating me," he mimicked, giving her a peck on the cheek.

"You're a history geek; that made it easy."

Sophie inwardly chewed on the relationship between her husband and daughter. There was growing tension between the two of them, the inevitable struggle between the blossoming young lady and the protective father who was having difficulty accepting her growing up. If she were honest, it was true for her as well. She gave herself credit for being supermom. She hadn't anticipated a souring relationship with her daughter as she reached her teens.

"It's going to pass, John. It's just the age when so much is changing, her body, her tastes, her interests. To a thirteen-year-old girl, there is no explanation for the tornado raging within and around her. She's not a child anymore, and she's not a woman. She needs time to understand who she is and who she is becoming, and we need to appreciate that and support her. I see so much of myself at that age in her."

"Honestly, Soph, I can't imagine you ever being as sullen and moody as Ann."

"I would stand in the mirror and practices my scouring expressions so everyone would leave me alone. Mamma kept a running list of what each expression and mood meant so she would know what reaction to have to the many temperaments of Sophia. She used to say since I was a Gemini, she needed to prepare for which twin showed up for the day."

"Yeah, but you didn't want to change your name to Adara."

"No, Scarlett. I loved *Gone with the Wind*."

"Creative people are different. We're all tortured souls," she chuckled, "but we have our gifts to rely on. We write and dance and sing our hearts out when simple conversations are insufficient. Look at her; she comes alive when she draws. It's good Ann has her art. I poured my heart and soul into my stories at that age, chiefly when I couldn't explain to anyone, let alone myself, how I felt. She's a good kid, John. Lighten up."

The crowds on the train increased as they drew closer to the mall. The intercom system announced each stop along the way, as more boarded and few left the train. The festive atmosphere on the subway system was contagious as an eclectic mix of people from across the country and around the world came to celebrate the nation's birthday. Independence Day, the day when members of the Continental Congress declared their freedom and liberty from the British.

We hold these truths to be self-evident, that all men are created equal, that they are endowed by their Creator with certain unalienable Rights, that among these are Life, Liberty, and the pursuit of Happiness.

I guess it wasn't self-evident to the founders that the people brought here against their will were also endowed with those rights, thought Sophie. *Life, liberty, and the pursuit of happiness; so basic, so necessary. I guess it's time to give Ann more space to chart her own path to happiness.*

By the time they arrived at their destination, there was standing room only on the train. Their stop was a familiar drop for many of the museums and sights of the city, so the crowd would disburse in a labyrinthine of directions once they were above ground. As they left the train, John and Sophie fell in step behind the kids. Sophie watched thoughtfully as her daughter walked slightly ahead of Josh and Emma.

"She doesn't realize it yet, but our Nubian Princess is going to break a few hearts."

John growled as two teenage boys passed Annie and glanced back, smiling and whispering. Annie peeked back slightly, but sensing her parents were watching, rewarded the smiles with a withering eye roll.

Sophie smiled and gazed appreciatively at how gracefully Annie carried herself, gliding as she walked. Dance lessons since the age of three gave her the posture of a ballerina. *She's a beautiful girl,* thought Sophie, *and a good girl as well.*

"Maybe it's time to change the routine a bit, John. We could be more spontaneous in planning, kind of cut back on the A-type personality stuff, the need for them to prepare research about everything we do all the time. We could let Annie bring a friend along or ask what she would like to do some weekends; even allow her to do something with her friends on occasion instead of expecting her to come with us all the time."

John stared wide-eyed at Sophie. "Annie?"

"She's growing up, John, get over it."

Puffy clouds floated above the clear morning sky, promising to morph into a typical hot and humid summer day, the kind for which the DMV was famous. As they exited the Metro at the Smithsonian Station at Twelfth Street and Independence Avenue, Sophie caught up to Annie and draped her arm around her daughter for the ten-minute walk to the memorial. She stretched to kiss the top of her head, appreciating that Ann was now nearly as tall as she. *She's going to be taller than me,* she thought.

"You certainly entertained Josh and Emma on the train with your sketchbook. May I have a look?"

Annie attempted to contain the horror-struck expression on her face as she inspected her mother's outstretched hand. With resignation, she handed Sophie the sketchbook. Sophie flipped the book open and gazed at the picture for a second, and then laughed.

"Oh, Ann, I wish I had had your raw talent and rich imagination when I was thirteen. I have no idea how you think of some of this stuff."

"It's the same way you think of storylines for your books," said Annie easily.

And there it was, thought Sophie observing her daughter, *the connection they shared as artists, the inexplicable link that most people never understood. The mystifying well in your soul that explodes in word, song, art, dance, and sculpture.*

Sophie inspected at the sketch again. On the page was a drawing of two Sankofas. John gave the kids a lesson a while back on the Sankofa bird to explain why history and heritage were so important. As he explained, the word *Sankofa* means 'go back and get it.' He often cited to the children a version of the proverb linked to the bird *"It is not wrong to go back for that which you have forgotten."* Not fully understanding the metaphor, or probably not wanting to, Emma repeated the phrase whenever she lost or left something somewhere, which unfortunately was quite often.

The legend of the Sankofa originated in Ghana in West Africa, revolving around the Akan people's quest for knowledge. It illustrates a bird walking forward, but its head is looking backward with an egg in its mouth. The simple meaning of the symbol is that one has to go or look back and understand where they came from to move forward toward who and what they want to be. The Akan people believed they were better prepared for the future by understanding the past. The egg in the mouth of the bird symbolizes a piece of knowledge or history.

In Annie's drawing, the two birds were sitting on the Metro, facing each other. In place of their heads were sketches of John and Sophie. The eggs in their mouths were Emma's and Josh's heads. Annie was standing over the birds with a giant net.

"I am amazed that you could have done all this in such a short time."

"I draw the four of you so much I can do it with my eyes closed."

"Well done, Ann."

"Well done, *Annie*," her daughter replied mockingly.

Approaching the memorial, Annie thought about everything that was happening around the city these days. She gazed back at the soon-to-open African American History and Culture Museum, then onward toward the King Memorial, then back again. She studied at the street where an African American President and First Lady had walked and waved to an adoring crowd after being elected, not once, but twice. Accomplishments in every field were reported in the media almost every day. So much acknowledgment of African American achievements. But her parents sometimes talked about racial issues as if there were still problems. *I don't get it,* she thought. *Things are great.*

The copper color of the museum gleamed in the morning light like a pyramid of shiny new pennies. The anticipated opening of the museum was a frequent topic of conversation in their home, and she had never seen her father so excited, and not just her father. Everyone in her family was eager to attend the opening in the fall, even Annie. She appreciated this was not just another museum of old stuff; it was the history of their existence in this country. An account that spanned generations. People would visit the city and take pride in the museum and the King Memorial. The memorial represented the Civil Rights struggle, but also the struggle to have Dr. King's likeness and contributions included in American history as a matter of course, not just as a battle about race to be fought and won.

As Annie lagged farther behind, she was gradually engulfed by her emotions, sentiments submerging her into a distant past beyond her experiences, a past where the humid breeze whispered her name. Calling her to a place of unseen spirits, spirits of ages gone by assaulting her senses as her heartbeat quickened. Her instincts told her she was an extension of these spirits. Gazing about at the sprawling four acres on the banks of the river, she wasn't quite sure where she was. It no longer had the appearance of the national mall. She felt a hazy consciousness of complete freedom, a freedom she understood her ancestors merely dreamed about, but confusion as well.

The sound of her father's voice broke the spell, and she rushed to catch up with her family. She joined them as they circled the statue making their way to the wall behind the mountain stones to read the quotes of Dr. King engraved on the structure.

- *"Injustice anywhere is a threat to justice everywhere. We are caught in an inescapable network of mutuality, tied in a single garment of destiny. Whatever affects one directly affects all indirectly."*

Sophie read the words then ran her hands over the carvings, momentarily shutting her eyes. Annie watched her mother. *She feels what I was just feeling.*

"Such powerful words, they speak to my spirit," Sophie said distractedly. Opening her eyes and gazing at the children, she smiled.

This inscription is from Dr. King's letter from the Birmingham jail.

Ordinary people say the most extraordinary things. Most people think the 'I Have a Dream' speech was Dr. King's most ardent oratory, but there were other speeches and conversations; some were never published, but they touched people's lives. That's the reason I try to impress upon you to be good listeners when you meet new people. Just as important, you must be careful with your own words.

Words have a force frequently underestimated. They can hurt or heal. They can educate or deceive. They can encourage or dishearten."

Annie watched intently at her mother. "Do you think Dr. King understood at our age that his words would change the course of history?"

"Who knows what he said when he was your age that helped other kids; what kind words he uttered to a new student in school, what brave words he pronounced that stopped a bully or inspired an introvert. You can't anticipate when you will meet someone who can transform your hearts with their words. Or maybe you can change theirs. It could be someone you've already met or a total stranger; it could be someone your own age, or it could be the words of someone who lived long before you were born. You just never know."

For a moment, Sophie appeared confused and distracted. Her brow furrowed as if she were trying to remember something crucial but could not grasp the thought. A quick snap of her head brought her back, and she smiled, grabbing Annie's hand.

They continued their walk, meandering through the 'mountain,' stopping to read the various quotations, and moving around to the front of the King statue. They gazed up at the colossal image, each lost in their own thoughts. *What is the garment of my destiny?* wondered Annie.

There were benches near the statue, and Annie sat and commenced drawing. Her hands moved carefully across the page as she etched her vision of the statue. Instead of Dr. King coming out of the mountain, she sketched the girl from the village emerging forth. Contrary to Dr. King's crossed arms, she drew the girl's arms outstretched. On the tips of her fingers was the Sankofa. She reflected on her mother's comments about the impact of words, knowing it was the writer in her speaking. She could identify with that; it was the same thing she experienced when drawing. Maybe her art would one day transform a stranger's mind or touch their heart. Too bad it didn't have that effect on her family. They didn't believe her about the girl, and she doubted this sketch would change their minds.

Annie cocked her head, examining her work. She was pleased with the first image and flipped the page. She sketched again, concentrating on the girl's face this time, her expression, kind but intense and fixated on Annie as if she wanted to tell her something, something important. She turned the page once more, this time, working just on the girl's face. She was young, but her face was fierce, filled with knowledge and wisdom beyond her years. She had high cheekbones; chipmunk cheeks. There was a gap in her front teeth, full lips, and magnetic eyes that called to you. Annie thought she was beautiful.

She drew her without the hat with a part down the middle of her thick natural hair pulled back. She sketched another in the dated clothing, careful with every detail. The skirt was a dark color, long, but not too long that you could not see the brown laced boots. She wore a wide belt around her waist. The white blouse had long sleeves, a high neck, and ruffles down the front. The straw hat was simple with a black band around it.

Annie was sure of what she had seen. Just like words spoke to Sophie's spirit, images spoke to Annie's. When they did, she could not rest until she captured it on paper. Annie drew that image, and like the girl's expression earlier in the morning, the picture reflecting back at her whispered, "I know you. It is not wrong to go back for that which you have forgotten."

Annie closed the sketchbook as her mother approached. "Dad and I are going to walk over to the information center. Keep an eye on Emma and Josh. We won't be long."

Annie stood and joined her sister and cousin as the two of them ran around the statue. She followed them to the rear and called to them.

"Hey, you two, let's take a selfie."

Pulling out her phone, they backed up to the statue. Holding the phone up and leaning on the wall, Annie urged, "Say Sankofa."

They uttered the word with giggles, but suddenly the rear of the wall moved backward and turned a full 360 degrees, and when they were again facing the split section of the mountain, nothing was moving. The world appeared frozen in place. People in mid-sentence were looking at one another but not seeing. There were no sounds, no voices, no birds singing. Annie whispered *Sankofa* again, and the wall turned once more. This time, it did not turn back.

Sold

At long last, the ocean voyage has ended. Herded from the ship like cattle, we comprehend the infinite capacity some men have for inflicting pain. The stench of the sea mingled with a composite of human scents penetrates the air. Our bare feet touch the ground of this alien land. The mournful jangle of shackles bears witness to our approach. Those who bother to gaze at us or acknowledge our existence do so with expressions of dispassionate indifference. They are devoid of all emotion. What more could be expected of men and women capable of accepting and profiting from the bondage of human beings. These infidels proclaim a belief in a God. Which God would that be? What merciful God would condone this evil. My spirit longs to tell the slave traders, slave keepers, and all who partake in or ignore this practice that they are doomed.

My countrymen hang their heads low as we shuffle along. I defy the sentiment that I must bow to these brutish men. I hold my head erect. I am met with a sharp blow for my perceived arrogance and am reminded that my survival depends on a portrait of submission and docility. My worth to them depends on their success in reducing me to emotional and physical servitude. I must appear subservient and humble. I drop my head, and they cannot see the contempt in my eyes. I am beginning to believe that it will be a struggle to hold on to my own human kindness and decency.

We are led to an open pen and made to wash each other down and plaster one another with oil and tar so our bodies will gleam and give the *illusion of health. We are fed mush in a vain attempt to fatten us for their human harvest. Foolish men. They believe they can erase the evidence of the infamous voyage; hide the marks of their abuse. I have shown more compassion to the animals that roam the plains of my homeland than these men have shown to fellow human beings. There appears to be no end to our trials and tribulations at the hands of these men.*

We are forced into pens and await the disgrace of being bartered like human commerce. Before the bidding begins, they strip us down to inspect us. They peer into our eyes and examine our teeth. They pinch our arms and touch our most private areas. They make us jump and run so they might surmise if we will be able to do the work, lift the load, breed more slaves. We are auctioned in lots and as individuals depending on our worth and the needs of the slave keepers.

I accept it may result in more distress, but I cannot allow this humiliation to proceed without reply. I claim my pain and my dignity as my own. I open my lungs and howl with one piercing scream as the auctioneer pronounces me sold.

Mamie

The wall revolved, and a brilliant spark discharged, compelling Annie, Josh, and Emma to throw their hands over their eyes. Startled, they peeked through their fingers, gingerly dropped their hands, and discovered they were standing on a dry, dusty country road. Enormous Georgia oak trees lined the narrow lane as far as they could see. A barbed-wire fence divided the path from a large grove of pecan trees. They spun around in unison to discover the wall was gone. There was no sign of the monument, no streets, no people, no evidence of civilization.

Turning back to the wide-open space, the three of them could not absorb where they were, how they got there, or what lay beyond the stretch of land. The barbed wire meant keep out, which was immaterial since they had no intention of venturing off the scant pathway or going beyond the periphery. But nothing else suggested people were near where they were.

What. Was. That." Josh surrendered to his tendency to stutter when he was nervous. "And-and-and where the-the-the heck are we?"

Exasperated, Annie slapping a gnat that landed on her arm and said. "I'm assuming this is one of Dad's elaborate living history lessons."

"Seriously, Annie? You believe Uncle John could pull off something like this; bring the world to a halt and make the buildings on the National Mall disappear."

"I know you think we went in a circle Josh, but obviously, they used technology to simulate what we experienced. It was an illusion. We saw a hologram or freeze-frame or whatever."

Josh blinked and flashed Annie a stupefied expression.

"Reality check, cuz. Logic dictates that not a word you uttered makes any sense whatsoever. What you are suggesting is not technically feasible in downtown Washington DC. We're outside, and the museum is blocks from here. Besides, how could Uncle John anticipate we would go to the rear of the monument and lean on an invisible trapdoor that no one else happened to prop themselves on? Where is there this much open space in the District except for Rock Creek Park? It's a museum, not an amusement park. No one does this kind of thing at a museum, and we should know, we've been to thousands."

"So maybe it has nothing to do with the museum or the monument. We just need to stay calm and stop sweating it. Mom and Dad are lurking somewhere out there laughing at us."

Breathing deeply, Annie surveyed their surroundings. Bending down, she skeptically examined the color and texture of the dirt, which was atypical for Washington. It was compact and red, similar to soil she had seen in the Deep South. She noticed a change in the atmosphere; hot and hazy, like DC, but different somehow. A scent of rusty red iron was in the air.

Annie had to give her parents credit; this was different. Time to play along. She hoisted her backpack and assumed access back to the Mall had to be here someplace. "Let's go," she ordered.

They pushed ahead, speculating on what this journey would ultimately involve. They imagined a host of elaborate and comedic scenarios matching John Sesstry's penchant for wild narratives. He was a prolific storyteller and prankster. The National Mall was prime material for his legion of fables. His position with the Smithsonian meant he was acquainted with the myths of the Nation's Capital, and he was an expert on the folklore of historic landmarks.

There were ghost stories and tales of magic about the mysterious Castle, the original building in the Smithsonian Complex, which was only a few blocks from the monument. Built in 1855, it sat on a large plot of land isolated from the rest of the city. Enslaved labor had been used for quarrying the sandstone used in its construction. Fire destroyed parts of it, but it was rebuilt to the specifications of the original facade. Over the years, government buildings and more museums were erected near the Castle, but that didn't diminish its prominence.

Always a movie buff, *Night at the Museum* and the sequels were among John's favorites, though he roundly criticized the one about the Smithsonian for its inaccuracies. The Castle was visible from the African American History Museum. Annie was willing to bet this was some convoluted Castle hoax executed by her father.

At length, an eerie silence, only broken by the occasional squawk of a bird, descended as they wandered the endless road. The trees were no longer close together, and the surroundings were more desolate than they had been at the outset. The three youngsters' apprehension mushroomed with every step as the stagnate heat began to take its toll. Even Emma, who rarely ran out of things to say, turned quiet. The feeling of isolation was growing insufferable. Though she didn't want to admit it to Emma and Josh, Annie found their circumstance more frightening by the minute. When he could no longer remain quiet, Josh mumbled cautiously, "This isn't right, Annie; we've gone at least three miles."

Emma was close to tears. "I'm scared, and I want to go back. We should turn around and go back."

With her voice quivering, she persisted in demanding they return to where they started. "Mom and Dad wouldn't do this to us. Some scary person is luring us to a dangerous place."

Annie snapped at her sister. "It's too late to backtrack. There's nothing to return to. We wouldn't even know when or where to stop." Steadying her voice, she added, "We cannot let our imaginations get the best of us. We are meant to move ahead. Of that much, I'm certain."

"Mom, Dad," she yelled, "we're tired, and this isn't fun."

She didn't expect a response, and she didn't receive one. She was worried about Emma, not just about her fear, but about the way she was sweating. Annie's mouth was dry and sticky, and they were all feeling the effects of the heat, but Emma appeared uncommonly flushed. Annie dove into her backpack to get Emma some water, but the plastic bottle she had loaded in her bag that morning was gone. Her phone was also missing. *Had she dropped it when the wall turned,* she wondered? Oddly, the sketchbook was still there.

"Where's your water bottle, Emms?"

Emma looked in her backpack, but like Annie, there was no water bottle. Josh searched his pack as well but found the same situation as his cousins. There was no bottle of water.

They plodded farther toward a bend in the road marked by a weeping willow tree. It stood out because it was different from all the others. A field of wildflowers grew nearby. Giving directions to Josh and Emma, Annie said, "We'll walk to that tree up there and sit down in the shade and wait for them to find us."

They rounded the bend, and to Annie's surprise, she saw the girl from the village sitting at the base of the tree reading a book. Resting on a blanket with her back leaning on the tree, the girl did not appear to be bothered by the heat and seemed not to notice the approaching children.

At last, Annie thought. *Really funny, Mom and Dad, you didn't see any girl, and now what are the chances of finding her here sitting under a tree in the middle of nowhere.*

"Hello," she called as they approached the girl. "I'm Annie, but I guess you know that already."

The girl did not raise her head from the book, as Annie continued, "This is my sister Emma and my cousin Josh," Annie said.

"Hi," Emma shouted.

The girl glanced at the threesome, her lips curved into a soft smile. "I'm so sorry, I didn't mean to be rude, but I was so taken by this here book that I didn't hear you."

She had a deep southern accent, and her tone was sweet and mellow, instantly comforting Emma.

"What can I do for you children?"

"I'm thirsty," complained Emma.

Smiling, the girl produced a canteen from a nearby knapsack and extended it to Emma, but Josh slapped away Emma's outstretched hand before she could take it.

"Has anyone else's mouth been on that?"

The girl tilted her head, glancing at Josh with amusement. Turning to Emma, she cooed. "Here, darlin', I think you ought to drink this. You're awfully flushed."

"Do you have another one?" Josh inquired.

"'Fraid that's my only one. You're welcome to have a drink as well, though, you too, Annie."

"Don't you have paper cups or something? This is very unsanitary. My mother is a doctor, and she says you shouldn't drink from someone else's glass or bottle because saliva transfers germs and viruses."

"A colored lady doctor," said the girl with pleasure, "Do tell."

She extended the canteen to Emma for the second time, who reached for it without hesitation. She took a small sip at first, but the water was fresh and cold, and Emma began taking large gulps.

"Stop, Emma," admonished Annie, "you'll drink it all."

"She's fine. There's plenty more where that came from," said the girl.

Emma had her fill, then handed the canteen to Annie, who drank freely. She never tasted water so good. She gazed at Josh and raised her eyebrows. Resigned, he took the canteen. His eyes bulged as he downed the delicious water. Annie, Emma, and the village girl laughed. They took turns and drank until they had their fill. It didn't faze them that the canteen never emptied. Annie reasoned nothing else about this experience was conventional; why should a canteen filled with endless, revitalizing water be the exception.

When the three sat down, Josh inquired if the girl worked for the museum.

"Ain't no museum around here. I work with my mamma on the farm, in the kitchen, and about the house. In September, I'm going up to Atlanta to Morris Brown College. I'm gonna study to become a teacher. I suppose this book will be a fine story to read to my students."

"You mean down to Atlanta," corrected Josh. "Atlanta is south of here."

"Do tell now. And just where do you reckon here is?"

Josh considered his answer, but Emma broke in before he responded and asked what book she was reading.

"It's *Peter and Wendy* by Jim Barrie. It's about a boy who never grows up."

"We know the story," boasted Josh.

"We've seen the play and a bunch of different versions of the movie. The last movie we saw about Peter Pan was *Hook.*"

The girl gazed at the trio with amusement.

"Did y'all know," she went on, "that Mr. Barrie's brother died when he was a young boy, and that's who Mr. Barrie had in mind when he wrote this story. His brother was Peter Pan, the boy who never grew up. His brother never died in Mr. Barrie's heart; he just went away to a magical place called Neverland."

As she spoke, she turned to study Josh, and he had the odd sensation that this strange young woman understood him like most others did not. He felt she could discern his innermost feelings about his father's absence, emotions he kept hidden, even from his mother. He sometimes pretended his father was not dead but away on another deployment or some other kind of adventure. It was a coping mechanism when the thought of never seeing his father again got to be too much. He had always loved the story of Peter Pan but did not know about the author's brother. *I guess it's better to think of Dad in Neverland helping with the lost boys. It would be more fun fighting Captain Hook than fighting in a real war,* he thought.

He looked up, and the girl was gazing at him with an expression of sympathy and understanding. Her soft brown almond-shaped eyes reminded him of his grandmother.

"Hey," exclaimed an exasperated Annie, "I understand you're in character and all that, but we need to find our parents. We've been out here for an incredibly long time, and we should be getting back to the Mall."

"I wouldn't worry about time if I was you; it works kinda funny here for visitors."

"And just where exactly is here?" pushed Josh.

"We're in Bibb County near Lizella, Georgia Josh. The town was named after the postmaster's daughters Lizzie and Ella. Ten miles from Macon, we're in the heart of Georgia, about eighty-five miles south of Atlanta."

Annie snickered at the expression on Factoid Josh's face. She wasn't sure what shocked him more, being told he was in Georgia or being corrected on his geography.

"I suspect, judging from your clothes, she continued, you might also want to know when you are, as much as where you are."

"That is nonsense," Josh protested. "If we're in Georgia, explain how we traveled hundreds of miles in an instant."

Emma glared at Josh, disapproving of his tone, and then turned to the girl. "We've traveled back in time, haven't we? So under the circumstances, being in a different place is about as normal as being in a different time. What year is this?" probed Emma.

"It's 1912."

Rolling his eyes, Josh turned to Annie for support, but she had stopped focusing on the discussion and was taking in the scene. She had removed her sketchbook from her backpack and was drawing a picture of Emma and Josh sitting at the feet of this peculiar girl. She was pleased with how well she had captured her at the Mall, but this was better. She wasn't drawing her from the memory of a quick glance. She was right here in front of her, almost posing for a portrait. The girl was lovely, and Annie wanted the drawing to reflect her ethereal nature.

"When did y'all come from?"

Emma was now all the way in. "When and where," she giggled in response. "We weren't in Georgia when we left. We came from Washington DC, but we live in Virginia. It's 2016 back there. And, I don't want to be rude, but I would like to return and use the toilet if you understand what I mean."

When the girl didn't respond, Emma leaned over and whispered in her ear.

"Oh, well, back there by that tree would be 'bout as good a spot as any."

At Emma's horrified expression, Annie put her pad down.

"I need to go too Emma, let's go together."

As Annie and Emma headed to the trees, the girl and Josh stared at each other.

"I reckon Josh is short for Joshua. My daddy's name is Joshua."

Josh nodded. "There's been a Joshua in our family in every generation since my great, great, great-grandfather," he replied.

"My, my, that's a lotta greats. You're fortunate to be able to go back that far in your family. You know, it's an honor and a big responsibility on your shoulders to carry an ancestor's name, especially amongst our folks."

"Why is that?"

"Well, we colored people have only been told a portion of our history; who we are and where our people came from in Africa is a mystery to most. Before the war, folk got bought and sold, some of them when they were especially young, and they didn't remember their mammas and daddies. Earlier than that, some died on the ships that brought them to America from Africa. They may have had family on those same boats that made it here but were then sold to other parts. We'll probably never know."

"When a name is passed down from one generation to the next, the one that gets that name gets the job of telling the stories of those who came before them, so all ain't lost."

"Annie's mom, my Aunt Sophie, is our family historian. She's done research on our ancestors, but she runs into roadblocks because the information available on slaves is uneven."

"I have an Aunt Sophie too," said the girl. "Be sure to learn as much about that first Joshua as you can so you can tell your children, and they can tell their children all about him. You know you have to look back to understand and appreciate where you came from before you can figure out where you're going."

Josh grinned, "Yeah, like the Sankofa." As he uttered the name of the ancient bird, he noticed a small lightning flash in the distance over the girl's shoulder. Slowly he stood up and whispered the word once more.

"Sankofa."

Again, there was a flash of light. He said it three more times with the same result.

The girl studied Joshua, "you know, my grandfather use to tell us a bedtime story about Sankofa."

Joshua yelled for his cousins, "Annie, Emma, get over here, I know how we got here, I think I know how we keep going."

His cousins were already approaching but hearing the panic in his voice; they started running.

"What are you shouting about?"

"Say Sankofa."

"Why?" Emma probed suspiciously.

"Do not ask why; just say it." Emma repeated the word, and Josh saw the lightning spark again. "Now, when I count to three, say it with me. One, two, three."

"Sankofa," they repeated together.

Just as Josh suspected, the flash expanded larger than the first time, and he caught a glimpse of a large white building with stairs cascading on the left and right. A horse and buggy were in front of the building. Within seconds, the beam and the opening disappeared.

"I know this sounds insane, but I think when the three of us said Sankofa back at the monument, we opened a portal for time travel. If I say it by myself, there's a tiny sparkle of light, barely noticeable. When you and I say it together, Emma, the light is bigger, and there's an opening way over there. The three of us saying it together caused a cosmic event."

They gawked at Josh, who stood his ground, nodding vigorously. Annie turned slowly to where Josh pointed.

"Sankofa," she whispered and saw the beam of light. Twisting back towards Josh, she held up her hand, and using her fingers, she signaled a count of three. On three, they both said *Sankofa*. They caught a glimpse of the light and the opening.

"We have to go over there," exclaimed Annie excitedly, "that's our way home."

"I'm not sure it's going to take us home. I saw a building, but it wasn't the Mall or 2016," said Josh.

"It doesn't matter. It takes us onward."

"Onward may not be what you expect, Annie," warned the girl.

Josh bowed slightly to her. "Sometimes you must look, or in our case, go back and understand where you came from to make progress and know where you're going." The girl smiled and nodded at him.

"That's fine, Joshua, that's real fine."

Annie, Josh, and Emma gathered their things.

"Be careful who y'all talk to. Try not to talk to any white folks at all, and if you do, don't look em in the eye. Drag out your words and try not to sound so proper."

They hugged the girl and trotted toward the place of the light. Josh turned and contemplated what to say.

Pointing to the book, he stammered, then found his voice.

"You know that place between sleep and awake, the place where you can still remember dreaming? That's where I will always love you. That's where I'll be waiting.

It's my favorite quote from the movie *Hook*. It's another version of *Peter and Wendy*. Anyway, I think about it when I miss my Dad. It's where I know he's waiting for me, and now I think you might be too one day.

For what it's worth. I think you'll be a great teacher."

"Thank you, Joshua."

Emma locked eyes with the young girl, "you never told us your name."

Tears glistened in her eyes. My name is Mamie, Mamie Calhoun."

The three of them gaped slack-jawed and wide-eyed at Mamie, who winked and told them it was time to get going.

They sprinted to the spot where they had seen the light. Annie glanced back one last time to wave, but Mamie was gone. "Well, guys, I think we just met our great-great-grandmother. Who knows what's in store for us next?"

Taking each of them by hand, Annie began to count.

"One, two, three."

Fox McElmurry

S queezing their eyes shut, the trio of youngsters yelled, "Sankofa!"

A gust of wind yanked them off their feet as they passed through an invisible vortex, leaving them on the periphery of a bustling nineteenth-century town. Throngs of people – black, white, young, and old - crowded together or moved along the dusty red road, attending to their daily routines. To their amazement, Annie, Josh, and Emma discovered their clothing transformed to the times of their surroundings. Their backpacks had changed and were now simple knapsacks. Annie thought about the missing water bottles and wondered if there was a connection between the bottles' disappearance and the travel through time. She wondered if whatever bewitchment guiding their travels prevented things out of place like plastic bottles and cell phones from going back in time.

They spotted the Crawford County Courthouse, identified by a sign hanging in front of the stately building Josh had observed from the other side of the portal. Other buildings were places of business. There was a general store, a blacksmith shop, a location designated as the US military headquarters, and the Office of the Freedmen's Bureau. There was a jail, unmistakable in its appearance and purpose. Mamie had told them their first stop had been in Bibb County, and the Crawford County sign verified they were probably still in Georgia. They visited Bibb County during a family reunion and learned it had once been part of the larger

Crawford County Seat. The military presence and the office of the Freedmen's Bureau were clues they were in a period sometime after the Civil War.

The facade of the town was a synthesis of the times. An observation of the townspeople told a story of residents rebuilding their lives and readjusting to the massive changes brought about by the war. By merely scrutinizing the appearances of people, their circumstances were apparent. Their demeanor reflected the influence the changing times had on them. The social and economic system for whites had been turned upside down by the Civil War, and now the administration of Reconstruction enforced even more changes. Blacks had always been poor in this still-young nation. Now they were poor but free and responsible for their own destinies. Most welcomed it; some were not sure what to do with it. Frightening and inspiring all at once, their circumstances had changed. Both assemblages were making their way in unchartered waters.

Well-to-do women wore full skirts and dresses made from silk and other delicate fabrics. Even on this hot summer day, the wealthier men wore long frock coats. The women and girls of more limited means wore homespun shifts made of coarse, durable cotton, covered by aprons. The men sported work shirts and pants or overalls. Hats and bonnets protected everyone's heads from the sweltering heat. Black women wore bandannas. Dust, stirred up by the movement of horses and carriages, covered everything.

The kids' eyes followed horse-drawn wagons with huge wheels carrying people and goods to an open market close to the courthouse where people sold and traded assorted merchandise. The stalls in the market held meat, fresh fruits, pies, and various jams and loaves of bread. Emma's mouth watered.

Satisfied that their garments were inconspicuous for the times, Annie almost led Emma and Josh forward but hesitated to approach the swarm of people. They were three kids from the twenty-first century, unsure of what to do when thrown back in time. Putting aside their simple attire, they could not alter the reality of being different from the Black people they saw. Their posture and the way they carried themselves radiated an air of confidence inconsistent with the newly freed Black people of this era. They innately projected an aura of worldliness and privilege incompatible with their surroundings. A change of clothes could not transform who they were or how they had been brought up.

Annie was unsure how much time had passed. They had not eaten anything since breakfast, and time had lost its meaning.

Emma was the first to speak. "I'm hungry."

"You're always hungry," responded Annie.

Josh, who was as hungry as Emma, sulked.

"Even if we had money, I don't think we could walk up there with a twenty-first-century Abe Lincoln five-dollar bill and buy lunch. Remember what Mamie said."

Mamie's warning rang in their ears as they scanned clusters of men and women divided by race. *Be careful who y'all talk to. Try not to talk to any white folks at all, and don't look em in the eye if you must speak to them. Drag out your words and try not to sound so proper.*

They knew one wrong move, one wrong word, could spell disaster.

"Well, we can't just stand here," Annie declared. We have to find a portal that will take us back to our own time. We found the first two passages by chance. Now that we know what we are looking for, we can focus on locating a portal. Sankofa," she whispered, turning around. Not surprised, she was still dejected when she didn't see a glimmer of light.

"I wonder what the connection is between Sankofa and our ancestors," Annie said. "It's no accident that the first portal took us to Mamie. This is about our ancestors. We locate another ancestor, ask the right questions to conjure the Sankofa magic, and enter a portal that takes us home. I may sound like Gramby, but we're here for the teachable moment. We learned some things from Mamie. One of us or all of us must learn a lesson from an ancestor here."

"It was easier in 1912 where Mamie was; it was only her. There's more than just one person here, and Mamie told us to be careful who we talk to," said Josh.

"True," replied Annie, "but I refuse to accept we are at this specific location at this specific time by accident. I trust that large brain of yours to help me figure this out. What were you and Mamie talking about when you observed the portal?"

"We were talking about my name. Mamie said it was important that I learn about the original Joshua in our family. Of course, I didn't know then we were talking about her father. She said I should tell my children about him so that they could relay the story to their children. Future generations should remember and appreciate where they or we came from. She repeated a version of the Sankofa legend like what Uncle John taught us. 'You have to look back to understand where you came from before you can move forward.' I said that it was the same as the story of the Sankofa; although there are lots of versions, the point is pretty much the same in all of them. As soon as I mentioned the word *Sankofa*, I saw the light."

"I think our purpose here is to learn about the family members who came before us, so we can honor our forefathers and mothers, our history, and our culture," stated Annie. "That meshes with the idea of finding another ancestor. Mom made us help her with all that census research for her books, so we know a bunch of names. Our predicament is how to identify a random ancestor among all these people."

They gazed around, considering their situation. They turned in the direction of the courthouse where a cluster of Black men was in earnest conversation. One man appeared to be leading the discussion as the others listened intently. He was well dressed and commanded the attention and respect of the other men surrounding him.

"Maybe we could ask him," offered Emma, pointing to the man.

"That there is Jefferson Franklin Long," interjected a voice from behind them. "He's a tailor here in Crawford County, but he's studying politics. Folks say he will be the first colored man from Georgia to go to the US Congress."

The three turned to see a woman smiling at them. She balanced a large basket on top of the turban that adorned her head. Emma could smell the aroma of food seeping from the linen-covered hamper. She closed her eyes, taking in the wonderful scents. Unconsciously she groaned at the sweet smells as her stomach growled. Annie jabbed at her with her elbow.

"Afternoon," she said. "I'm Mary McElmurry, and who might you be?"

"I'm Annie Sesstry, and this is my sister Emma and my cousin Josh."

"How do you do?" said Emma and Josh in unison.

"Are you headed anywhere in particular?" asked Mary.

They didn't know how to respond, so the three of them remained silent.

"Well, it's fine to meet you, Annie Sesstry, and you too, Josh and Emma. You young'uns tur like you been traveling a while. Me and my family was fixin to have lunch over in the grove. There's a plenty food, and y'all welcome to join us if you like."

Annie hesitated, but Josh loudly whispered, "she's a McElmurry. Besides, Annie, we're hungry."

Cutting her eyes at Josh for his boldness, Annie bobbed her head. "Thank you, that's very kind of you; lunch would be great."

Mary scanned the group of men and, catching the eye of one, and gave a short wave. He said something to the others and walked toward Mary and the trio of visitors. "That be my husband, Laverne 'Fox' McElmurry," Mary pronounced with pride.

Astonishingly Annie counted on her fingers as she thought, *and if that's the Laverne McElmurry I think he is, that be our great-great-great-great grandfather.*

Fox was tall and solid. His hands were calloused, and he walked with a slight limp but his smile was warm, and his coffee-brown eyes were filled with humor and kindness.

"Well, Mary, who have we here?"

"Mr. McElmurry, this here is Annie, Emma, and Josh."

"How do," said the man.

"Hello," the three replied.

Annie felt compelled to say, "My real name is Ann, but people call me Annie."

"These young'uns gonna join us for lunch Fox."

"All right now," he grinned.

Taking the basket from his wife, he gestured to their guests to follow. Fox and Mary strolled toward an open field surrounded by wild Blackberry thickets. The drone of bees and other summer insects assaulted the wild grasses, and a smattering of trees provide shelter for a crowd of picnickers. Annie, Emma, and Josh fell in behind them. Mary's voice was low, but Annie could hear the whispered conversation between the two adults.

"Y'all mighty bold gathering out by the courthouse like that."

"I told you we was gonna register to vote today, Mary, and that's what we did."

"We's free, Fox; don't mean we's safe. That Freedmen's Bureau and Union League ain't gonna protect us late at night from that snake Alden James and the rest of his kind."

"I ain't fraid of Alden James, and I intend to vote when the time comes, Mary. The likes of James can't accept the outcome of the war, and they's gonna keep trying to stop progress. But we been through too much to stop now. We got to be the ones to take charge of our future. We can't count on General Lewis and them folks from up North to stay round here forever or to make a difference here in Georgia by themselves. This is our home. We got to vote and get the right people to run this here state and this here county. Colored people got to be more than free Mary, we got to be equal, and there's a big difference between the two.

And what about you gathering up stray chi'ren," he said with a wink.

"Are they who I think they are?"

"Somebody got to gather them up 'fore Alden does. Anyways, haven't had the chance to ask these much yet, but judging by their nerves, the way they talk, and the way they just sorta came outta nowhere, I reckon they are."

"Strange, never had more than one at a time before," mused Fox.

"Uh-huh; that troubles me some. Makes it harder for them to blend in. Colored folks is nosy enough, let alone white folks from up North and the ones from round here. The war left a heap of bad feelings, and this Reconstruction has caused plenty of mistrust. These ain't good times for visitors, Fox. We gotta get these chi'ren back where they belong before something happens. Why would the Unknowns send them now?"

"When has it been a good time for us to receive the Travelers Mary? 'Fore the war, we had to hide em to keep someone from thinking they was runaways. Now, we got to keep 'em away from the likes of Alden James, but then again, we got to keep all the orphans away James and those who just can't accept that slavery is over and done with, and they don't get to own folks no more. As for us, well, we don't get to pick when and how the story is told. We have to make sure it gets told. Now relax. We've had visitors before, and they've always gone back."

"They've always left," recounted Mary sarcastically. "We just hoped they went back where they came from."

Listening to the conversation between Fox and Mary sent a shudder through Annie. *We're not the first-time travelers,* she thought. *That's good; they're familiar with the portals and where we find one. But who is Alden James and who is the Unknown, and how is he or she the reason for us being here?*

They reached the grove, where several families were preparing to eat. Some meals were more plentiful than others, many as simple as potlicker and cornbread, but the mood was upbeat and hospitable, and no one appeared to notice Mary's three guests. A band of children rushed to greet Mary and Fox as they arrived.

Mary smiled. "Annie, Josh, Emma, these here are our chi'ren. That there is Ann, holding baby Frances. Ann is sixteen. These others is William, fourteen, Mary Jane, eight, Cicero, ten, Henry, six, Amos, four, and Missouri. She's two.

"Hey," the children chorused.

"Hi," Annie, Emma, and Josh replied.

"Now y'all get to knowing one another," said Fox.

Mary set up lunch with Mary Jane and Emma's help. The boys played and became acquainted with Josh. Slipping his glasses into his pocket, he caught on quickly to the game of marbles the boys played and, in fact, won a round. Annie was surprised at Josh's easy comfort level with new people, something that didn't always happened. She relished seeing him so carefree with other children. Something about his encounter with Mamie had affected him; lifted the cloud of sadness that always seem to follow him, at least temporarily. She took out her sketchbook and began drawing. The elder Ann sat down beside her. Though her skin tone was darker than Annie's, the two girls were strikingly similar. Annie scrutinized her ancestor and recognized the reflection that gazed at her from the mirror earlier in the morning. Ann peered over Annie's shoulder and examined the sketch of Josh playing with her brothers and the other boys.

"Your drawing is real good."

"Where y'all from?" the older Ann asked.

"Virginia," replied Annie.

My daddy's from Virginia, but he don't know his people up there. You go to school?"

"Sure," said Annie.

"All y'all go to school?"

"Yeah, she chuckled, we all go to school."

"Do you read good?"

Annie stopped drawing and closely examined her great plus aunt. "I love to read and draw. I've kept all my books, even those I had when I was little. Books and pictures take you all over the world."

Glancing down at her drawing, she continued. "Sometimes, they take you on extraordinary adventures through time."

"You got books of your very own?" the older Ann asked incredulously.

"My mom's a writer. I've had books my whole life."

"I ain't had no schooling, but I know my letters. We don't have no books at home, 'cept my mamma got a Bible. Can't nobody read it, though. Mary Jane and Cicero gonna go to school in September. The Freedmen's Bureau and the American Missionary Association are settin' up two new schools for colored children. One is Lincoln Elementary School, named for Mr. Lincoln. The other one is Lewis High School, named for General John Lewis, the head of the Freedmen's Bureau over in Macon. Mary Jane and Cicero going to school, and they gonna help me read after they learn."

"Why aren't you and William going to school? Won't they allow all colored children to go to school, now that the war is over?"

"Papa says, Mamma needs me at home to help with the younger kids. William gotta help Papa in the fields. Ain't no time for us to go to school."

Ann glanced at her parents to see if they were watching. When she was sure they weren't paying attention, she bent her head close to Annie and asked softly,

"Was you born free?"

Annie hesitated, then meekly nodded her head in the affirmative.

"Mamma don't like us to talk about who born free or not. I ain't never met no colored girl born free before anyway, cept baby Frances here, so I don't see why speaking on it matters. Them white people from up North talk about lots of colored chi'ren born free. I think Mamma don't want us to think they's better than us. Mamma says God made all our souls free from the very beginning, and that's all that matters now. But I think if I was born free like those colored kids up North, I would'a been reading a long time ago, and it wouldn't be so hard to learn now."

Annie swiped a tear from her face and reached out and hugged the girl she was named for. Both girls began to laugh. "You'll get better at reading. And I have a feeling that books and schooling are going to be very important in this family."

The lunch Mary prepared was tasty - fried chicken, ash-roasted potatoes, cornbread, and the best lemonade Annie, Josh, and Emma ever tasted. They ate as if it were the last supper, and Mary was visibly pleased they enjoyed her cooking so much. For dessert, they had sweet potato pie.

"This pie is so good. It tastes just like my grandmother's," sighed Emma.

"Folks used to ask why I was always tipping round Mary Gaines," said Fox. "I'd tell 'em 'cause she made the best sweet potato pie in all of Crawford County."

Mary threw up her hand and smiled at her husband.

"Maybe your grandma's recipe was passed down to her. Where she from?"

"Our Gramby Rose Clarkson grew up in New York, but her mother was from Georgia," replied Emma without giving her comments much thought.

Fox and Mary smiled at each other. Annie took a sneak peek at Josh, who now had his glasses back on, and nodded.

Annie sketched as they sat and talked. She drew the family scenes in the grove. People eating, laughing, talking. Children playing. *Not so different from a family picnic during a Calhoun-McElmurry family reunion,* she thought. At last, Mary signaled it was time to gather their things. As they cleared their surroundings and packed up, a woman passed by, stopping and staring at Annie, Josh, and Emma.

"Hey Mary, how you?"

"Just fine, Clara."

Mary's voice was calm and strong, but Annie noticed her back tighten and a slight quickening of her breath.

"Whose chi'ren are these?"

"Kinfolk from Savannah," Mary answered without hesitation.

"Humph, you sure got a lotta kinfolk from Savannah."

"Peoples living all over since the war ended Clara; trying to find work, looking for family. Sometimes they got to leave their kids for a bit. I ain't got no more family all about Georgia than anybody else. Even you I spec."

Clara examined Emma up and down. "You's a pretty little thing; how long y'all gonna be here?"

Over Clara's shoulder, Emma saw Ann put her finger to her lip shaking her head. She dropped her chin to her chest without answering.

Clara then turned her attention to Josh. "Well, look at you with spectacles and all."

"You got someplace to be, Clara, 'cause we do."

"Touchy ain't you Mary?"

A tense silence descended on the group. When no one spoke, Clara stared at the family and moved on, taunting Mary with a final, "Y'all have a nice day now."

Mary stood erect and watched the woman leave, but Annie could see her fortitude dissolve as she exhaled.

"Old devils never die. You know, I don't care much for Clara and her meddling, and I care less for her no-count man Isaac. Alden

James' daddy was the overseer on the Willard Plantation before the war, and them boys come up together. Hear tell Isaac turned on his own more than once to curry favor or save his hide. This ain't good, Fox. She gonna run to Isaac and Lord knows who else and tell 'em about these chi'ren. Who knows who gonna come snooping around after she starts blabbing her big fat mouth."

"Calm down, Mary, you gonna scare these chi'ren, and there is nothing for them to be 'fraid of." His eyes crinkled as a broad smile spread across Fox's face. "Josh and Emma, why don't y'all help Mary and the others pick up." Sweetie, you take the young'uns home. Josh, I think it best if you put your spectacles in your sack till you get to the cabin."

He stared at Annie for a moment shaking his head at the wonder of it all. Grinning, he slowly enunciated her name. "Ann Sesstry. That is a right unusual name. Well, Miss Ann Sesstry, I' speck it's time we took a walk and had a talk about some other kinds of ancestors."

Alden James

One hundred and seventy-six years before Annie, Josh, and Emma traveled through time to Crawford, County, Georgia, the lives of four other children intersected in a manner that would ultimately affect the Sesstry-Cooper journey in a most unanticipated way.

Alden James was eight years old in 1840, on the day he fully comprehended the differences between him and his friends Isaac and Jenny. It was the day that would mold his character, or some believed, shatter his decency. It was the day he learned people were assessed by the color of their skin and by where they ranked on society's ladder of privilege, the hierarchy of status, success, and wealth.

Alden was a handsome boy. He had chestnut-colored hair that coiled to his collar, and he sported a perpetual grin that showed off his baby-doll dimples, a grin that was warm and affable and always welcomed Isaacs's friendship. Creative and carefree, he invented new games to play with Isaac. They explored the land, climbed trees, and swam in the Ocmulgee River, though teaching slaves to swim was forbidden. Slaves who could swim were considered escape-risks. Moreover, their scents could be lost if they traveled by water.

The idea of running was not a concept that Isaac ever entertained or fully understood at his young age. He simply enjoyed the company of his friend Alden. But this hot August day would be the last anyone would see Alden's sweet smile. Alden would surrender his innocence, and his friendship with Isaac would change forever.

Isaac was two years younger than Alden. He had daily chores in and around the house, but he did not work in the fields. His liberty from fieldwork was not because of his age but because he was often forgotten about and invisible to those in charge. He was fortunate, as fortunate as an enslaved boy could be. He lived on a plantation with many laborers, so the work was shared, and children could be spared in some measure in their younger years. His father was sold before he was born, and he was orphaned when his mother died in childbirth. He wandered about the slave quarters and the plantation with little supervision. As a baby, he had been passed from one mammy to another. It was nothing short of a miracle he had survived his early years. The women did their best to care for Isaac, but he wasn't anyone's responsibility, and each had their own burdens to shoulder. His skinny frame was a testament to his meager diet and general neglect.

Despite his hardships and young age, Isaac was sufficiently clever to move about unnoticed unless he was doing something wrong. His lack of restraint and discipline gave the illusion of an actual childhood, and he spent his spare time playing with Alden. The boys did not discuss Alden's freedom or Isaac's bondage. It was the certainty of their existence, and neither had experienced any other way of life. They had played together throughout their brief childhood and not once did either boy give thought to the differences in their circumstances until that day in August.

Alden and Isaac, along with Jenny Willard and her slave Bessie were playing by the Nickajack Creek. Bessie's mother, Cage, cared for Isaac more than most, so Bessie and Isaac were often together. Cage was skilled at sewing and weaving, giving her a position in the house. She planned to teach Bessie the skill to keep her out of the fields as well. Blacks in the field had a harder life and a shorter lifespan than those who worked in the house. Though, working in the house carried tribulations of its own.

The four youngsters played as children do, forgetting temporarily that their friendships were taboo, forgetting so completely as they splashed on the banks of the water that their laughter drowned out the sound of the galloping horses approaching the creek.

Jeffery Willard and AJ James were searching for Jenny when they heard the laughter and trotted to the creek where the children played. Jenny's father, Jeffery, owned the Willard Plantation, which he inherited when his father died two years prior. He was groomed to assume the position from a young age, and when his father died, Jeffery slipped easily into his calling as family patriarch. He was a shrewd businessman and commanded the respect of landowners in Crawford County and throughout Central Georgia. Some in the elite planter class believed Jeffery would one day run for governor of Georgia.

Alden Joseph James Sr. was the overseer for the Willard Plantation. He went by the nickname AJ and had a reputation for being mean and abusive, not just to the workers he managed but to his wife and children as well. Like Alden and Isaac, Jeffery and AJ had known each other their entire lives, but devoid of childhood fantasies, they did not view one another as friends and certainly not equals.

Jeffery and AJ were the same age. Both were white Southern believers of the racist doctrine of white superiority over Blacks, justifying slavery, but there the similarities ended. AJ spent his days in the fields managing the dozens of enslaved workers planting and plowing the Willard land. His weathered skin, sun-streaked sideburns, and workers' clothing made clear he was not part of the gentrified class. His pinched eyebrows gave the impression of being suspicious of everything and everyone. The whip hanging from his saddle symbolized authority.

AJ lived in a two-story farmhouse built with the help of free labor available on the Willard land. He could read enough to do his job but never developed an appreciation for reading for the sake of knowledge. His position as overseer of the plantation afforded him the income and privilege many whites lacked; nevertheless, large-scale landowners ruled the South, and AJ was not of that class. He harbored no illusion that he ever would be.

The aristocratic life led by Jeffery gave him the youthful appearance that came with privilege. He lived in a white-columned antebellum mansion epitomizing prosperity and status in the South. He was educated and well versed in the ways of the world. He savored his position in life.

Jeffery's horse scarcely came to a stop before he dismounted and grabbed his daughter by the arm. Jenny Willard was the plantation princess. The only female offspring of Jeffery and Amy Willard, she was spoiled and pampered. She was not exceptionally pretty, but with money came the advantages of beautiful clothes and proper training. The reflection of grace and Southern feminine charm was evident even at a young age.

"What exactly do you think you are doing, Jenny? Your mother has been calling for you, and half the household staff is out searching."

"We were just playing," the child pouted

"You don't play with coloreds and…"

Grimacing at Alden, he hesitated before speaking. He was not inclined to call the boy what came to mind, at least not in the presence of Jenny, whom he considered too young to hear certain phrases.

"People outside your social standing. Appearances are of the utmost importance. Bessie is your slave, and you may play together in the house when she is not working, but that is the limitation of your association. Is that understood?"

"Yes, daddy," answered Jenny.

His anger on clear display, Willard turned to AJ, "I thought you raised your children to have better sense than to step out of their place AJ."

"Sorry, Mr. Willard," he mumbled.

Putting Jenny on his horse, Jeffery Willard admonished coldly, "don't let it happen again."

"Bessie is supposed to stay with me in case I need something," protested Jenny.

He turned to the young Black girl. "Bessie, get yourself back to the house this minute. Your mamma's gonna skin you alive for your part in this."

Willard road off with Bessie running behind them toward the plantation house. Isaac and Alden attempted to run as well, but AJ grabbed both boys. Nostrils flaring and shaking with rage, he drew Alden close to him.

"You want to be a niggra?" he seethed. "I'll treat you like a niggra." He pushed the boys to the ground, grabbed the whip from his horse, turned, and struck them both twice across their backs. Isaac screeched in pain, but Alden crawled away from his father, turning to stare at him, first in shock and then with undisguised malice. He would not give his father the satisfaction of crying. AJ lifted his arm again, but Alden grabbed the end of the whip. He held tightly to the burnished leather ignoring the sting to his hands.

Alden hissed at his father. "Jenny ain't no niggra, and she was here too."

AJ shook his head, laughing at his son with contempt.

Didn't you see the way that man looked at you? You ain't good as Jenny Willard, and you never will be in that man's eyes. You best learn to stay in your place. We all have a place in this world, Alden. Niggras," he said, glaring at Isaac cruelly, "ain't entirely human and are at the bottom of humankind. Poor, landless whites ain't much better, but at least a step above them kind. Whites like me who work hard and own a small piece of land, ain't got much, but we make decent money and rest in the middle. The rich, high-class folks like the Willards are at the top. I do all that I can to follow that order and keep up in my class, and I won't have you messing that up. I won't have you acting like poor white trash, one step above a coon."

Turning to Isaac, he said, "You step outta line again, Isaac, and I'll see to it you get sold. Ya understand?"

"Ya, sir," answered Isaac through his tears.

"Don't nobody care about you, boy. Nobody would even notice if you was gone. Tomorrow you have yourself in the field picking cotton, or I'm gonna whip the skin off your hide."

AJ left the boys kneeling by the creek.

"Alden, I's sorry you got hit 'cause you was playing with me."

Alden haughtily shot back, "shut your mouth, boy, and you call me massa."

Isaac wanted to laugh, but instinct kicked in, and he cautiously moved back from Alden.

"You ain't no massa."

"But I will be, best believe I'm gonna be on top. Ain't gonna be no overseer the same as him either; I'm gonna be a massa." I'm gonna be better than him. I'm gonna live in that big white house."

Alden got up, spat on the ground, and walked off, leaving Isaac weeping by the creek. It was the last day of their innocence and their friendship.

***

As time passed, Alden and Isaac became adept at using each other. Isaac took Alden's verbal abuse because he had no choice, and occasionally it could get him out of the fields when Alden insisted to AJ that Isaac was needed to help him with something. Alden relished having someone to abuse and taunt. "Did you know some niggras get to be overseers? You behave yourself, and maybe I'll let you be the overseer on my plantation one day." Isaac did not take the bait, responding to Alden with an occasional, sarcastic "ya sir massa."

Through the years, Alden watched his father and observed Jeffery Willard. "Ain't gonna be no overseer like AJ," he recited on a regular basis. "I'm gonna live in that big house, ride in a fancy carriage and marry Jenny Willard." He took any opportunity that emerged to learn and practice reading.

He balked if anyone referred to him or called him young AJ. He would demand that everyone call him Alden.

"AJ is what you call an overseer," he once told Isaac. "Alden or Mr. James is what you call a massa. Ain't gonna be no overseer. I'm gonna be a massa."

Alden didn't venture far beyond the plantation boundaries on his own, but from time to time, he was permitted to ride into Knoxville, Georgia, with his father and Jeffery Willard. He trusted in the presumption of his dreams and nurtured them by observing men conducting business in the county seat. He regarded the way they spoke, the way they walked, and the way they dressed. Most of all, he watched the way they negotiated the sale of commodities and people. Cotton and slavery flourished in Georgia, and Alden believed all he needed to achieve his dreams was to work and save enough money to buy few acres of land and a few slaves to start his business, and it would grow from there. Most whites in the South did not own slaves, and those who did owned fewer than twenty. The Willards were the exception, holding more than one hundred men, women, and children in bondage.

Alden believed he would marry Jenny Willard someday and combine his land with her father's. It had been the fantasy that occupied his waking thoughts and governed his actions. Her two brothers were lazy and showed little if any interest in learning about cotton, rice, or slaves. Alden would share his aspirations with Jenny, who hung on his every word. Men didn't talk to women about business, so Alden's willingness to confide in Jenny was unusual, and she rewarded him with her unabashed adulation. Jeffery might not think Alden was good enough for Jenny, but she was smitten and would not be kept away from him.

Jeffery took note of Alden's efforts and took the burgeoning apprentice under his wing. He didn't envision Alden marrying his daughter but knew he could utilize the youth's ambition and hard work.

When Alden was old enough to go out on his own, he found it difficult to raise the money or borrow enough to purchase a sizeable piece of property. Landowners in pre-Civil War Georgia fiercely protected their property rights and were reticent about selling any of it unless they needed to and except at the highest price and to those already in their social circles. Jeffery Willard did not offer Alden assistance in becoming a local landowner for fear it would further encourage a relationship with Jenny.

Alden was not deterred from his goals even though he found it difficult to secure work that would give him the kind of money he needed to buy land and attain the lifestyle he so desperately sought. Unrest was growing in slave quarters, and the use of slave patrols was increasing. The patrols were groups of civilian men who scrutinized the actions of the slaves, searched their homes, and stopped and questioned them about their activities, especially at night. Alden, couldn't conceive of Georgia without slaves and didn't believe patterrolling, as it was called, was a long-term solution, but there was money to be made.

Abolitionists and the slave insurrection movement was rapidly expanding all over the South, including Georgia. Movements such as the Underground Railroad grew legendary and Blacks, inspired by the tales, took off in search of freedom. There was more than enough work for the patterrollers, and it paid well, more if a runaway slave was captured and a bounty had been offered.

For shrewd patterrollers such as Alden, there was an added financial advantage of having information that went beyond the mere comings and goings of slaves. He launched a devil's partnership with his childhood comrade Isaac to obtain the smallest pieces of intelligence that might give him an advantage over the competition.

If there were rumors of uprisings or suspected locations of runaway slaves, Alden would find ways to get Isaac's workload reduced in exchange for news of what was happening. At first, he passed it on to the patrol leaders, but soon found a way around them and went directly to the landholders who funded the patterrollers. If something went missing or was stolen from a plantation home, Alden knew who was buying and who was selling, and whether the money was being used to pay for the resistance. When he was unable to intervene on Isaac's workload, he paid him a small sum of money for reliable information. Cotton was king in Georgia, but information could be just as valuable when used in the right way; it could increase a man's wealth. It didn't take long for Alden to become a patrol leader with growing influence throughout Central Georgia and beyond. It took just a little longer for Isaac to become a full-on traitor to his people.

In 1860, Alden saw his growing prosperity threatened by the election of Abraham Lincoln and further with Georgia's secession from the Union on January 19, 1861. Most of the white men of fighting age in Georgia went off to fight with the Confederate Army, including Jenny's brothers. Never one to follow the crowds, Alden went to sea, but not before convincing Jenny Willard to be his bride. He served on a blockade runner until his ship was beached. Serving in the Confederate Navy was dangerous but highly profitable. As the single lifeline to the outside world, those who served on the Confederate ships were rewarded with high pay – Union, not Confederate currency. They had access to Black market goods denied

Confederate soldiers and civilians. The bounty Alden brought home to Jenny superseded anything her father or her brothers could offer.

When he returned home, Alden moved into the big house and started to run what was left of the Willard Homestead. He and Jenny already had one child, and it was not long before there was another on the way. Alden had miscalculated the pull of freedom and the subsequent determination of the Union Army. Sherman's March to the sea and Lee's surrender at Appomattox Courthouse destroyed any hope he had of being a slave master, but the lessons learned as a slave patroller, a sailor, and a black-marketer laid the groundwork for the next steps in his quest for wealth, if not respectability. In 1867 when Annie, Josh, and Emma arrived in Crawford County, Alden had a thriving business.

The Travelers

Annie cast a glance at Fox as they drifted away from the picnic. Absorbing the implausibility of it, she recounted her astonishing day. *I've traveled back in time and met my great-great-grandmother. I had lunch with my grandparents from four generations past. The kids Josh and Emma are playing with at this moment are our ancestors, great-great-great-aunts, and uncles. On top of all that, my name is Ancestry.*

Monitoring the cluster of people, Annie marveled at the sight of Emma and Josh blending in as if they belonged. They do belong, she thought; these people are our family.

Fox and Annie strolled aimlessly through the main thoroughfare of Crawford. Continuing to take stock of her surroundings, Annie was still not quite able to take it all in. These were the buildings, the people, the sounds and smells of the Georgia that existed one hundred and thirty-six years before her birth.

Fox's deep baritone voice interrupted her thoughts.

"Well, Miss Ann, tell me about yourself."

"What do you want to know?"

"Well, to start with, where you from?"

"Virginia."

"I come from Virginia too, but I don't think either of us was planning to leave home when we did," he said softly. What year is it back in your Virginia?"

Surprised at the directness of the question, she answered with equal sincerity. "2016."

"My goodness, I can't fathom the world that far away in time."

"I heard you talking to Mrs. McElmurry. You've met others not from here, not from now, Isn't that right?"

"I have, but not as far forward as the twenty-first century. You are the first. What's it like?"

"It's very different from here. Automation and technology affect all aspects of our lives. There are machines of all kinds. Machines are a part of everything we do. They take us places like your horses and buggies, but without animals, with the push of a button or the turn of a key. Cars and trucks, and buses travel on the roads. Airplanes soar in the sky. Machines wash our clothes and cook our food and do the dishes after we're done eating."

Catching the apprehension on Fox's face, Annie pulled out her sketchbook and rapidly drew. "There," she said triumphantly, pointing to each item, "a car, a plane, and a phone." She then proceeded to explain each article as best she could to a 19th-century Black man.

"Nearly everyone carries a phone," she pointed to the one on the page. "We talk through them, and we can talk to whoever we want, whenever we want. We have computers. Smartphones are computers, but we also have laptops, desktops, and tablets as well. The phone takes pictures too, and you can see them and send them to someone right after you take them.

"I had my phone when we left, but I lost it when we came through. I would take your picture to show my mom and dad, but since my phone is gone, I did it the old-fashioned way; I drew you." She held up the pad so that Fox could see his likeness. He chuckled with pleasure.

"Draw the computer."

"Drawing it wouldn't explain what it does. It saves and stores information. Some programs let you do a mountain of things. You can play games, write letters, do math, and find information on anything."

"Can the computer locate people, and tell you where you come from?"

"Sometimes, it depends on what information has been entered into the computer. Nowadays, almost everyone's birth and death are entered into the public record, but that wasn't always the case. The information that comes out is only as good as what goes in."

"What about America, Annie? How different is America from what you see here?"

"America is the most powerful country in the world and has all the devices I mentioned and more." We have, and we've sent a man to the moon if you can believe that."

That was unbelievable to Fox, but it wasn't the technology or the gadgets that interested him.

"What about the Union? Does the Union hold after the war? Are the state fully reunited? I guess what I'm asking is, are there still thirty-six states?"

"No."

Annie paused for effect as Fox frowned. Then she grinned.

"There are fifty states, five territories, and the District of Columbia. All thirty-six states stayed in the union, and fourteen joined later." There have been wars with other countries, but no more civil wars."

"Fifty states, my, my," said Fox with wonder. "And what about coloreds, are they treated same as white folks?"

Annie considered the question momentarily and frowned. "Everyone is supposed to be equal, but some people still don't like people who don't look like them, and it makes it hard sometimes. It extends beyond Black and white now. The kids at my school are from families from across the globe and speak dozens of languages. There are many cultures and traditions, and blending all those customs can be tricky if you understand what I mean."

My, how elegant she talks thought Fox.

"I guess if any come from Africa, it's by their own choice now."

Fox and Annie were so engrossed in conversation they didn't notice Jefferson Long as he approached them.

"Afternoon Fox."

"Afternoon, Jefferson."

"Who have we here?"

"This here is kin from Savannah. Annie, this is Mr. Jefferson Franklin Long; Jefferson, this is Ann Sesstry."

Casually closing the sketchbook, Annie extended her hand. "How do you do."

Long arched his brow and blinked at her outstretched hand before accepting it. Startled by the firm handshake, the confidence, and poise of the young girl, he was surprised and pleased at the way she looked directly at him and smiled. "I'm well he said, "how are you?"

Fox interjected before the conversation got out of hand. "Annie grew up playing with her master's daughter, who loved playacting. She would practice being a high-society lady on Annie and have Annie do the same; thought it was funny to hear a slave talk like that. Ann, you shouldn't act uppity with your elders child," Fox cautioned gently.

"Fox, don't scold the child. She wasn't acting uppity, and there is no shame in good manners. Colored children need them as much as white children. He observed Annie once again and beamed. "It's been a pleasure meeting you, Miss Ann."

The pleasure was all mine," Annie smiled."

Subtlety, Jefferson Long studied Annie as she and Fox moved on. The hair, skin color, that carriage; Master's child concluded Jefferson. One of the lucky ones that was given a broad swath, just as I was. Still, even under those circumstances, this young girl was unlike any colored girl, free or slave, Black or mulatto that he had ever met. He respected Fox's protection of the child. Not everyone took kindly to children like Ann.

Others stopped to greet and chat with Fox. Annie meandered along the main street of Crawford County, observing the surroundings as he talked with friends and neighbors. She was startled when a white man came up behind, grabbed her arm, and sneered. "I haven't seen you around her before, girl. Where you from?" The man's tone and expression were menacing, and a frightened Annie wrestled to free her arm. "I'm talking to you, girl. I asked, where you from?"

"Afternoon, Mr. James," said Fox as he gently pulled Annie toward him. This here is Annie, my kinfolk from Savannah."

"That so," drawled Alden, how did she get here to Crawford Country?"

"Oh, you know sir, a little walkin' a little ridin'."

"She don't seem like the kind that walks much."

Alden didn't wait for a response from Fox. He merely moved along after looking Annie up and down.

Jolted by the encounter between Alden and Annie, Fox took a moment to regain his composure before returning to his discussion with Annie. As they walked ahead, he warned her. "Don't wander off, Annie. It ain't safe everywhere around here. And be careful when people speak to you. Even kind folks like Jefferson Long. This ain't the twenty-first century. You need to put that book away. Not many colored children have books to read or to draw in. Most colored people are poor. The last thing they have to spend money on is books of any kind, much less drawing books."

Calm once again, he resumed his questions about the United States of the future. "Jefferson is going to run for Congress. I guess they have coloreds in Congress by now where you're from."

"There aren't as many as my parents think there should be, but yes, there are Blacks in Congress, and the President is, as you would say, colored."

"The President of these United States is colored?"

"Of these United States, fourteen more, five territories, and the District of Columbia, she teased. He's the first, and his name is Barack Obama." Right now, the campaign for the next election is going on, and one of the candidates is a woman."

Fox stared at her.

"A colored president with an African name. And a woman, you say. I guess that means women can vote."

"Of course they can vote," she uttered with slight indignation. "We have women, including Black women in Congress. Women hold a slew of offices. There are women governors and mayors. And some women are police officers and serve in the military. There are lady lawyers and doctors too."

"Well, don't get all riled up now he chuckled. These women must be highly educated. I'll bet your mother is educated."

"My mother has a master's degree, and Josh's mother is a doctor."

Fox grinned. "Well, I guess you can say education is very important in your family."

"Education is really important in our family," Annie said softly. You and I, we're family. I'm pretty sure you are my great-great-great-great-grandfather."

Fox explored every inch of Annie's face, determined always to remember every feature and characteristic of the young continence. He cupped Annie's face and remarked, "I had a feeling there was something there; I just wasn't sure what."

"How is this possible" asked Annie. "How can we be here? How do we get back?"

Fox took a deep breath. "You were summoned here. You're what we call a Traveler baby girl. They got them in lots of families, colored families, anyway. They're charged with finding out the truth about their unknown ancestors. Sometimes they go to their own family members, sometimes to other people's families in other times searching for clues. When we happen to meet one another, we share what we know; names, places, kinfolks. You're one of the few I've met from my own family. The only one, in fact, directly descended from me. There's one Traveler in every generation of traveling families."

"Well, it appears that there are three in my generation," said Annie.

"I'm still trying to figure that out. I'm not sure Emma and Joshua were meant to be here. Travelers take their first journey, sometimes their only journey, after their thirteenth birthday. Joshua and Emma aren't old enough to be Travelers; they happened to be with you at the time you were called."

"Called by who?"

"Called by our Unknown Ancestor. I was a Traveler too, Annie. Maybe the first one in our family. I don't recollect my mother and father. Don't know if I had brothers or sisters. I was born on a plantation in Virginia, and I was a little boy when I got sold to a slaver here in Georgia. I don't recall much about that awful day. I do remember hearing my mother hollering and begging them not to take me, but hard as I try, I can't remember her face. I was scared and lonely when I came here, and I never got over leaving my mamma.

"Round about my 13th birthday, I figured I might run away and try to find my way back to where I had come from. Guess I was too desperate or too stupid to realize I had no notion of how to get to Virginia, and even if I was able to run, I wasn't running to freedom. If I had made it to Virginia in one piece, they would have brought me right back here, and things could turn out worse for me if that were possible. But back then, I figured maybe if I could at least see my mamma once again, it would be worth it.

"Anyways, I was sitting with my back against the barn plotting my escape when I fell back on a loose board and found myself in what I fathomed was the pit of hell. I was on a boat, a ship, really. That ship was a rocking back and forth, and I thought I would be sick or maybe even die. I heard the whistling wind above, and I knew that ship was in the midst of a storm.

"I smelt the human waste and illness. I never before or since smelled anything so rotten. I was so closed in; I could scarcely breathe. All around me was chained bodies laid out side by side. It was so dark; I couldn't see; couldn't make out if the people were men or women. They moaned and cried and coughed. Someone reached out and grabbed my hand. I tried to pull away, but they wouldn't let me go. I was shocked at the strength of that grip. The person spoke to me just above a whisper in a language I'd never heard, but I understood what they was saying, and I remember those words to this day."

"I am not known to you, but I am a part of you, and my spirit summoned you here. I have been taken from my land, sold like chattel. I will never return home, never again see the faces of those I love. My family will never know what became of me. My descendants will not know my name unless you tell them, for you are one of them."

"What's your name?" I asked.

"Before that person could say another word, there was a loud clap of thunder, and fear coursed through my body. The ship's captain or one of the crew came down the steps. He was shouting and some of the slaves on the ship started to scream. The screaming drowned out the voice of the person speaking to me. I kept asking for a name, but the ship kept on rocking, and them folks kept on howling; I fell back against a post, hit my head, and woke up back at the barn."

Annie held her breath as she listened to Fox with rapt attention. She wanted to shut her eyes and push away the image of the slave ship and its sorrowful cargo. Her body was stiff, and her ears were ringing. She wanted to put her hands over them and block out his words. She didn't want to hear any more, to imagine what her unknown ancestor experienced on that revolting journey across the Atlantic Ocean. She didn't want to know what this stately man standing before her endured when he was enslaved; didn't wish to harbor the image of what the other Ann withstood for the first fourteen years of her life before enslaved people were freed.

"How did you get the name Fox?"

Fox peered off into the distance and relaxed into the warm memories of an old friend.

"When I first came to Georgia, an old guy named Amos took me under his wing. Taught me how to work the fields and made sure I got water and something to eat. Said he hoped somewhere, someone was doing the same for his boy. Told me if I was gonna survive, I needed to be smart bout things, have a backup plan when I was up to something. Be sly as a fox, he'd say. Well, I didn't hanker to the name Laverne too much, no how, so I started having folk call me Fox, and the name stuck. Later I got bought by Mr. Henry Newsom, but by then, I was Fox McElmurry through and through."

"Why isn't your last name Newsom?" she asked.

"I met a Traveler who once thought all of us were named after the slavers, but not so many slavers gave their surnames to slaves. Lots of folks held by slavers never even had second names. The census lists one name in their records for most coloreds. After the war, some freedmen just picked out a name they liked. Lots of Lincolns, Grants, and Washingtons. Truth is, I'm not sure how I got the McElmurry name, but I sure didn't need to be a Newsom, though I know some colored folks who are Newsoms."

Annie was familiar with the stories of abuse and humiliation that enslaved people suffered, but she was also taught in school that some slave masters were better than others. Gingerly she asked, "Was Mr. Newsom, a kind slave owner?"

Fox's face hardened. "Would a good man take a child from his mother's arms to hold him in bondage for free labor? No man can claim to own another man and call himself good or kind, or Christian, no matter what he tries to tell himself, Annie. Slavery was evil, and those who spread it allowed it and partook in it are foul devils who belong in hell. They let their sons die for the right to own another child of God. No matter what the Good Book says, I won't ever forgive or forget them. Henry Newsom did one decent thing. When he died, his will declared that his slaves be divided among his children, but it stated that families had to be kept together. We was bequeathed to his son Madison. That's how Mary and I got to stay together and to keep our children. Even then, I was never sure if Madison would abide by his father's will and keep his word not to separate us. Mary and me lived in fear every day that someone would break up our family. When the war came, there wasn't much time to swap slaves, so I never had to find out what Mr. Madison would do.

I worked on his plantation until Mr. Lincoln said I was free, and General Lee surrendered to General Grant. Now I'm a share-cropper on Newsom's land. I share what I grow, but he pays me some too. It's not much, but I don't work for free no more. The day will come when I own a portion of that land."

Annie had more questions, but her probing was interrupted by the tolling of bells and the sound of Mary's voice yelling for Fox.

She ran towards them, screaming.

"Sweet Jesus Fox," she bellowed. "They's gone. Snatched in the light of day. Mary Jane and Emma is gone."

What's In a Name

You do not yet know my name. The slaver has hidden it from the generations. It is incumbent upon you to bring it to light.

In my homeland, one's name is one's story; a journey into the past, a glimpse into the future. Much thought is given to the naming of a child. It may tell of the day she was born or the tale of a great ancestor. It proclaims the position of his father or the joy of her mother. The elders are consulted. The grandmothers give their blessings. One's name is one's destiny.

I long for the customs of my people, celebrations, and ceremonies that mark momentous occasions. Such is the naming ceremony for each new life. The naming ceremony is a rite of passage and a day of importance within the tribe. There is a great celebration on that day, and at its end, women gather around the fire and tell stories about the festivals that were held in honor of the birth and naming of their children. They bury the umbilical cord of the newborn beneath a common tree where others have been buried to connect us to the family and remind us we come from the earth.

The naming ceremony comes eight days after the birth of the child. The delay is to be sure the child has come to stay. I had come to stay, but on a dark day, the slave trader took me from my village.

Here in this land, I have no traditions. The slaver paid money and took me to his plantation. He falsely claimed me as his property, but I am no man's property. With no more thought than is given to naming a cow, I and others in my state were given a name or, rather, an alias. If I *hazard to try and keep my family-given name, I will be beaten until I utter it no more; what they elect to call me is but a single word. Do not be misled by the lore that tells the tale of the slaver bestowing his surname on me. He no more wishes me to carry his name than I wish to bear it. This mindless slaver supposes he can erase my essence if he erases my name. But I know who I am. I know what my parents called me. There is power in a name, and I will not relinquish that power. My name, my power, lives on in me.*

Each day before the sun breaks over the horizon, I fall on my knees and call on the Creator for the fortitude to forge through the abuse and servitude of the day. I petition the Architect of the Universe to protect those I love, calling each by name. I pray they remember me in their supplications and that no life-cycle ceremony for the dead is held for me, no final chants of my name. At last, I rise from my prayers and claim my spirit. I whisper my true name.

Hijacked Freedom

Emma and Mary Jane held tightly to each other. They understood they were in the back of a wagon, moving fast, but that was all they knew. Mary Jane knew of the child-snatching that had gone on since the end of the war. Emma, on the other hand, was unaware this was a common practice, but she did know being grabbed by strange men was not good. Neither child fully comprehended the extent of their troubles. The suggestion that they had been snatched by people who were kidnapping Black children and selling them did not spring to mind. But the truth was, slavery was alive, if not well, even after the Civil War ended, and Emma and Mary Jane were its two latest victims.

Slavery in the United States was born in Colonial Jamestown. It grew up during the Revolutionary period and matured in the era of Industrialization. Its very existence made a mockery of the Declaration of Independence and the Constitution, the sacred documents of the nascent country. Nevertheless, it had been a significant driver of the US economy, especially in the South, and even war couldn't put an end to the determination by some depraved people to buy and sell free labor.

Emma and Mary Jane's predicament was analogous to the failure of the US to solve the dilemma of slavery at the beginning of the country's history. If Annie had truly understood the circumstances leading up to the Civil War, she would have better understood Fox's questions about the Union. The Founding Fathers debated the issue of slavery but were unsuccessful in reaching a satisfactory resolution that would grant freedom to those held in bondage. It would take seventy-six years to end slavery, but not without constant skirmishes. The idea of slavery was contrary to the principles of the new country from its beginning, and the doctrine grew more intolerable as an increasing number of Americans challenged its legality and morality. Most enslaved people were unaware their fate was the source of debate and consternation. They merely knew their circumstances were intolerable. The odds of decreed freedom grew more elusive for Black men, women, and children in the South; thus, rebellion and civil disobedience spread. Moral outrage, civil unrest, and slave insurrections seemingly had no impact. The dependency of the Southern economy on free labor was too powerful, and the condemnation of slavery fell on deaf ears.

Abraham Lincoln was elected President of the United States in 1860. Fearful the Republican Party with its newly elected leader would abolish slavery, South Carolina, led seven states in seceding from the Union. Four other states would later join them. The citizens of these states renounced their country, established a government, and formed a new republic, calling themselves the Confederate States of American. Ironically Lincoln's plan was not to end slavery but to restrain its expansion to more states. The Southern states, however, did not trust Lincoln, and in April 1861, the Confederate States of America fired on the US fortress, Fort Sumter, South Carolina. They captured the garrison and began a Civil War, lasting until 1865.

To end the war in 1862, Lincoln signed an executive order, The Emancipation Proclamation. The Confederates were given a choice; end their rebellion or expect the government to discharge the executive order on January 1, 1863. The South refused, and the Proclamation was executed. It is a misconception that the Emancipation Proclamation freed the slaves. The Confederate States considered themselves a sovereign nation, no longer a part of the United States subject to its laws and executive orders. Theoretically, the Emancipation Proclamation would not apply to the states in the Confederacy unless and until those states were restored to the Union. Nevertheless, the Proclamation did have an immediate effect.

It altered the purpose of the war from saving the Union to abolishing slavery. It labeled the Confederate States of America a slave nation and the United States of America a liberator nation. Furthermore, it permitted slaves to enlist and serve in the Union Army, increasing its manpower strength, thus hastening the end of the war. Nullification of slavery came with the passage of the Thirteenth Amendment to the Constitution in 1865.

The Civil War claimed the lives of more than seven hundred and fifty thousand men. One-fifth of the South's male population died in the so-called War between the States, though not all died in battle. Some died of starvation, others of disease; a few met their demise as a result of the downright stupidity of their actions. Nevertheless, they were gone and numbered among the casualties of war.

The nation mourned and buried its fallen soldiers from the North and South, but the Spirits of the Unknowns mourned the loss of the millions of enslaved Africans and their descendants who died in the bygone years. They anguished for progeny held in bondage for two and a half centuries. They mourned the six million men and women who died during the Atlantic crossing, known as the Middle Passage. They wept for the loss of Black babies born to enslaved mothers. Half of those babies died of malnutrition in their first year of life. They mourned those murdered and maimed when they attempted to escape to freedom. They yearned to comfort the broken-hearted, separated from their children and families, sold to places and people on far-off plantations, never to see them again. They mourned those who had no one else to mourn for them.

There were Southerners who grieved for more than the loss of human life. The loss of money, prestige, power, and slaves weighed heavily on them. They lamented the abrogation of their way of life. Jeffery Willard could be counted among that lot. Believing in the supremacy of the Confederacy, he invested emotionally in the war and financially in Confederate bonds. He lost most of his fortune, though he held on to his land. His sons returned home from the war, broken and incapable of contributing to rebuilding their family's prominence. They had not added to building or maintaining that prominence and never anticipated or planned for life without slaves. They were, in effect, useless. Jeffery had opposed the marriage between his beloved Jenny and Alden James, but he had to admit that Alden had always been enterprising and was one of the few men who came home from the war with more than when he left.

The cost of the conflict, along with Lincoln's "new birth of freedom" for Blacks, brought poverty and destitution to a region of the country that had amassed enormous wealth galvanized by cotton, rice, tobacco, and most decidedly, free labor. The Southern economy was now shattered. The elite planter-class that had not experienced hardship before the war soon found it difficult to adapt and recover to circumstances so wholly altered. Those attempting to recover understood their way of life could not be restored without money.

If there was one thing Jeffery was sure of, it was that Alden James was adept at making money even under adverse circumstances. Alden would survive, and he would thrive. By attaching himself to Alden's coattails, Jeffery would also thrive. Jeffery needed Alden for the resurgence of the Willard name and fortune. If the price of that resurgence was Jenny, then so be it.

Alden had made a lucrative living, capturing runaway slaves in the years before the war. In the Confederate Navy, he consorted with Black marketers, yielding to his weakness for shady operations to boost his income. Now with the conflict over, Alden was not primed to relinquish his newfound status to farming and sharecropping for poor landowners, even his father-in-law.

He despised men who had never done a decent day's work yet still manicured their fingernails and bellyached for days gone by. They were in their present position d because incompetent rebel generals couldn't whip the Yankees. They lacked the backbone to stand up to Northern carpetbaggers descending on the South like locusts making up new rules for Southerners. They let Yankee generals strut around their towns like they had inherited the earth. Those men expected scoundrels like him to restore the natural order and believed they would then reap the benefits of the efforts of others. He would restore order, but he would be the one to reap the benefits. The current circumstances presented challenges, but none that were insurmountable. And with challenges came opportunity. The solution was what it had always been, free labor.

The Thirteenth Amendment abolished legalized slavery, but a new form of servitude and oppression was introduced by those who benefitted from the custom of slavery in the past and were shrewd enough to change with the times.

After the assassination of Abraham Lincoln in April 1865, Reconstruction ushered in the plan to rebuild the South, but neither the region nor America was prepared for four million freed Negros. Poverty teemed throughout the South among Blacks and whites, but the conditions for Black people were extreme. Black Codes established by landholders in the aftermath of the war were constructed to limit opportunities, suppress freed Blacks, and control cheap labor. The occupying Union Army did little to stop the Codes. Organizations such as the Freedman's Bureau and the American Missionary Associate had been created and dedicated to supporting those newly freed, but the tasks were overwhelming and the numbers too high. Those most at risk were children and teens lacking family members to care for them and guard their safety.

During the chaos, Alden built a network of unsavory characters willing to take risks to make money. Under Alden's leadership, they grabbed displaced young Blacks without families with the intent of selling them back into slavery. They moved them across state lines, making it difficult for them to be traced or even missed. Sold to whites who still wanted free labor, they wound up working on plantations and in domestic positions, in much the same way they had before the abolishment of slavery. With no money, no family, and no education, many stayed in place, at least for a time, because they had food, shelter and knew of no other life. When and if they outgrew or tired of their circumstance and mustered the courage, they left. The difference from their prior lives was papers were unnecessary to move about. What was the same for some was the fear that kept them bound to their masters. But when they chose to leave, no one stopped them or went after them. Nobody complained about their missing property because slavery was now illegal. Alden didn't object because it increased his business, and with Isaac's help, his supply chain was plentiful.

If ever there were a man at odds with his inner demons, it was Isaac. He was a compromised and damaged man without family or attachments. The former slaves of the Willard Plantation scattered, but Isaac had nowhere to go, and no one invited him to join them in search of a better life. From his early years, he bore the scars of abandonment, loneliness, and fear. After the war, he did what he had always done. He turned to Alden. Strangely, the two men were comrades, battling unseen forces for their own brand of survival. Alden was the one constant person in Isaac's life. When there was no one else, there was Alden. Lacking guidance and any other role model to set his moral compass, Isaac slipped easily into Alden's unscrupulous operations.

Alden road throughout Crawford County and the surrounding areas making contacts and negotiating the sale of the contraband. He left the kidnapping to others, not wanting to be seen with unfamiliar Blacks, particularly children. People suspected the truth about his business but could prove nothing of his enterprise. Though Alden's men were uncomfortable with Isaac's presence, he refused to exclude him. He trusted Isaac and was smart enough to know he needed someone in the Black hovels to get information and reduce the chances of grabbing a child or woman with ties strong enough to draw the attention of Blacks and Northern interlopers. Isaac and Alden knew taking children with close relations would invite trouble.

Isaac had help on his side of the operation. A woman named Clara from a plantation in nearby Macon was his companion. Nosy by nature, Clara kept her eyes and ears open for information that could lead to new finds. She was familiar with most of the Black families in and around Crawford County, and she helped Isaac locate children and girls who could be taken without a commotion.

Isaac and Clara's relationship was one of convenience. Commitment was difficult for Isaac, but Clara was the closest thing he had come to a romantic relationship. She was, for all practical purposes, his only connection to his own people. For her part, Clara found security in Isaac. Not emotional security, because developing emotional security was chancy during slavery. It could be too easily exploited. Clara's attachment was financial. The more money Isaac had, she reasoned, the more she could benefit.

Deep down, Isaac was ashamed of the man he had become and of the role he played helping Alden steal and sell his people. He languished in a place of self-denial, rationalizing that children who were like him - without family roots and lacking security - were better off on a plantation where they had food and shelter. Still, he knew what they were doing damned his soul for all eternity.

Clara had no such pangs of conscience. Women who had been enslaved suffered greater indignities than their male equivalents. They were used sexually by their slavers and overseers, worked in the fields as forced labor, and demeaned by the mistresses of the homestead being forced to nurse other women's babies before their own. They bathed and dressed the mistresses and cleaned the waste from their chamber pots. No humiliation was too great or too small. Bitterness coursed through their bodies and spiritually mutilated some beyond repair. Clara was one such person.

She also had another reason for helping Isaac. She wanted to find her daughter. Clara had given birth to two children. She had a baby that died soon after he was born and a daughter who was sold when she was seven years old. In exchange for her help, she made Isaac promise to help her find her daughter. He was to learn the names of all the girls taken who would be about her daughter's age now. The odds were long that Clara's daughter would be found, but she was out there somewhere, and Clara would spend her life trying to find her. She didn't care who she hurt in the process since no one cared about her pain.

Clara was eager to tell Isaac about the three children with Mary MacElmurray. She disliked Mary and considered her uppity with her husband and all her children. No one had ever sold one of Mary MacEmurry's children, she mused. She didn't believe for a minute those new children were related to them, and if losing those children mattered to Mary, Clara didn't care. She suspected Fox had insisted Mary take in some stray kids he had found. He was known for doing that sort of thing until he and the men he consorted with could find a place for them. If Alden's men took those three children, he would be doing Mary a favor since she already had too many mouths to feed.

Clara told Isaac about the children, who in turn told Alden. Alden recalled seeing Annie earlier and was sure she wasn't orphaned. He was also convinced she would bring a good price. He didn't mention that to Isaac, knowing he would object to taking any children associated with Fox. He gave instructions to his men to grab the children. He didn't anticipate they would capture Fox's daughter as well.

Snatching the girls had been easier and came quicker than anyone thought. Late in the afternoon, Mary Jane and Emma wandered away to pick Blackberries, and two of Alden's men grabbed them. The men didn't see the boy but assumed they could get him later. They tossed them in the back of the wagon and went on their way. Neither Isaac nor Alden were around when Emma and Mary Jane were taken. They were to meet up with the men at an agreed-upon location to get the children.

Isaac's knees nearly buckled when he saw Mary Jane McElmurry. He knew right away who she was but forced himself to ask, "Ain't you Fox McElmurry's baby?" Mary Jane looked at Isaac and lowered her eyes. Emma, on the other hand, stared brazenly at the two men.

"The two of you are going to jail for a very long time. My father will see to it. Right after my great uncles beat you up."

The men were startled by Emma's directness. Neither had ever been in the presence of a colored child with such backbone, especially under the circumstances such as these.

"My father knows some very powerful people in Washington DC, and you will not get away with this. You need to take us back where you found us and let us go."

Isaac backed away from the crazed child. "They got to go back, Alden. This is real trouble. One of em belongs to Fox, and who knows where this one come from. Wherever it is, she ain't no orphan."

"It's too late," said Alden. They know who we are. They get sold, or they die."

Go Down Moses

The color drained from Annie's face and her knees locked as Mary's words sank in. Fox sprinted, despite his limp, toward the clapboard building that served as the Black church in Crawford County. His children and others had already started to gather. Mary was close on his heels, and Annie, in shock, trailed them both. Terror gripped her as beads of sweat broke out on her face. The church was little more than a shack with weathered benches made of large pieces of timber. There were no backs on the benches, and the sweltering heat caused steam to rise from the dirt floor. Bolting into the church, she searched for Josh. When she caught sight of him, she ran and embraced him fiercely; she tried to stop his shaking. He jerked back and looked plaintively into her eyes. "I can't lose anyone else, Annie," he cried, "not again."

She did her best to soothe her younger cousin, cooing and whispering to him. "We'll get her back, we will get her back," she said emphatically, but he was reliving the nightmare of losing his father, and her words could not penetrate his misery.

More people arrived at the church, and the men joined a group huddled in conversation in a corner where they could not be heard. Jefferson Long was among them, and so was General John Lewis, the head of the Freedmen's Bureau. He was the sole white person in the crowded church. The women came in and took their seats, instinctively drawing their children close. Haunting memories etched their weary faces as the cruel flashbacks of fractured families surfaced.

Approaching Fox, the men gathered around him. Mary jumped to her feet. "We have to find Clara. She's the cause of this. She saw Annie, Emma, and Josh and thought they was orphans that her scum of a man could make money off of."

Stillness descended over the room, accentuating the hot stale air. The scent of the human sweat of the day penetrated the atmosphere.

"Hush now, Mary," Fox implored. "We'll get 'em back."

But his words rang hollow to Mary's ears. "You know I'm right. Everyone here knows I'm right. Clara and Isaac ain't here, is they? The bell rang, and they ain't here." She sank into her seat and groaned as sorrow overtook her.

Women reached to embrace her and stroked Annie as well, but Josh shrank from their touch. As Annie tried to make sense of what was happening, a man advanced to the pulpit and began reading from the Bible. She wanted to scream. Her ears were buzzing, and the sound was so severe she couldn't make out the man's words. People around her were nodding and moaning and rocking. She felt as if she were going insane. Struck by the lunacy of the situation, she almost giggled. She lowered her head, shut her eyes, and balled her hands tightly into fists. "Please, God let this be a bad dream, let it be a nightmare. Please let me wake up."

Another wail from Mary pierced the air, jolting Annie's eyes open. Knowing it wasn't a dream, she gave into her despair and wept. She aimlessly reached for Josh's hand as she gulped for air, hiccupping through her tears. She pierced her finger on a splinter from the old bench and caught a small piece of wood under her skin. The moaning and groaning grew more forceful around them, and a faint foot-stomping started, becoming louder with each thud of the men's work boots until the room shook with rage and madness. The pastor began "raising a hymn," the old practice of call and response, with the leader singing the first few words or lines of a spiritual and the congregation responding.

A woman slid next to Annie and put her arms around her shoulders to comfort her, but pulling back, Annie was having none of it. "This is a waste of time," she hissed. "Why aren't they searching for my sister and my - and Mary Jane instead of sitting here singing and groaning like wounded animals."

"We's just waiting for the right time, baby, don't you worry."

Annie yielded to the woman's offer of comfort and slumped into her arms.

The first hymn ended, and Fox stood to lead the next one. He focused pointedly on the woman holding and stroking Annie.

"Go," thud, thud, thud. "Go down" thud, thud, thud.

> *Go down Moses*
> *Way down in Egypt land*
> *Tell old Pharaoh to*
> *Let my people go!*
> *The church responded.*
> *Tell old Pharaoh to*
> *Let my people go!*
> *When Israel was in Egypt land*
> *Let my people go!*
> *Oppressed so hard they could not stand*
> *Let my people go!*
> *So, God said: go down, Moses*
> *Way down in Egypt land*
> *Tell old Pharaohs to*
> *Let my people go!*

Fox's eyes bore through the woman holding Annie. He sang louder as he continued to stare at her, and the church answered repeatedly,

"Let my people go"!

Annie turned slowly to the woman.

"Do you know where my sister is? Please, if you know, please tell me. I need to take her home. I'm responsible for her; she trusts me to take care of her. I need to take her home." Tears streamed down her face as she stared desolately at the woman. She slammed her hand against her chest and spoke louder. "She trusts me."

Dispiritedly, the woman held Annie's and Josh's attention, stroking each of their faces. She took a handkerchief from her pocket and wiped Annie's tear-stained cheeks. Sighing heavily, she kissed each of them.

"Don't worry; you'll take her home."

The woman stood, focused on Fox, and nodded imperceptibly. She turned and left the church.

The sound of the church hymn followed the woman out and down the dusty road, echoing through the trees for over a mile, just as the old spirituals had followed her throughout her life. They had followed her in the fields. They had called to her through the open windows of the plantation house where her mother taught her the art of weaving to take her from the fields. They followed her on the day she walked away from that plantation, a free woman. It was a song of joy on that day.

Her mother was gone now, but my how she could sing. Her haunting voice ringing like an angel throughout that plantation. Yes, the music was always there, just like it was this evening. In days past, it was used to maintain the rhythm of work in the fields; to teach the enslaved their new language and a new faith. Ultimately, it became a code sending out information, especially about quests for freedom and slave uprisings. Her mother said colored folks had learned to use the music against those who held them captive. She had taught her about Harriett Tubman using *Wade in the Water* to warn runaways to travel in and near the water to keep hunting dogs from picking up their scent. Yes, music had many uses for slaves and, now, for free men and women as well. They still needed a way to speak in code around the white man.

Two men, George and Nunn, had been at the church and were sent by Fox to watch over the woman. They discreetly fell in step at a safe distance behind her as she continued on her journey. Piercing heat from the red Georgia clay seeped through her thin-soled shoes, but she hardly noticed. She had traipsed this way hundreds of times. When she got her freedom and left that plantation for the last time, she swore she wasn't never going back. But here she was, passing by these old rotten shacks, not fit for human souls, but still the place she once called home. The place her mamma had tried to fix up as best she could with broken junk tossed out by those wicked white women.

The sounds of early evening, mosquitoes whining, and the hind legs of crickets chirping away, quickened as she climbed the broad steps of the plantation house. *Fancy me,* she thought, *walking right up to the front door like a lady visiting her friend and using this big brass knocker that I polished every day. Ain't so shiny now, is it?* She hesitated for a moment, then hammered at the door. When there was no answer, she banged away again, only harder.

A haggard woman holding a crying baby answered the door, another small child stood by shyly holding the woman's skirt. A third ran past his mother into the arms of the former slave who bent to welcome him.

"What do you want, Bessie?"

"Evening, Miss Jenny."

Bessie smiled at the boy she had stooped to greet. "Hey there Jacob, how you be?"

"You coming home, Bessie?"

"No, Jacob, I just come for a little visit."

"I asked you what you wanted, Bessie."

Bessie gently pushed Jacob away and stood tall facing the woman she had served from the time she was old enough to carry and empty a chamber pot until the day she gained her freedom.

"Two colored girls have gone missing. I thought Mr. James might be able to help find them. One of em is not from round here, but the other is Fox McElmurry's little girl. They's from over at the Newsoms'."

"We don't know anything about any missing colored children." It sounds like you need to check over at the Newsoms' place."

Flustered by the crying baby, Jenny blurted out, "she's just so colicky. I don't know what to do."

"If you'd like, I can make a little gripe water. It always helped when Jacob was a baby."

Jenny Willard James stepped back and let Bessie into the house who moved with such familiarity into the kitchen it was as if she had stepped back in time. She mixed the concoction and took the baby from Jenny. She dipped a clean cloth into the mixture and let the baby suck on the cloth.Back and forth, she dipped as she sang softly to the baby until she stopped crying. A few minutes later, the baby was asleep in Bessie's arms, and she handed her back to Jenny. She patted Jacob on the head and moved through the house and to the front door before Jenny could order her to use the back entrance.

Bessie turned to Jenny one last time as she reached the front door. "You have real pretty babies, Miss Jenny. I bet your heart would break into tiny little pieces if anyone ever stole one of them from you."

Bessie was at the bottom of the porch stairs when Jenny called to her. "Bessie, AJ has an old barn back of his place. I don't know what goes on there, but someone might want to check it out. They shouldn't wait too long. Things move fast from back there."

"Thank you, Miss Jenny, thank you much."

Bessie hurried back down the road to where George and Nunn waited. "They's in a barn back of old AJ's place."

"I want to go with you to get my sister."

A startled Bessie turned to see Annie standing just a bit further down the road.

"Sweet Jesus, Annie, Fox, and Mary are going to be more worried than ever now with you gone too."

"I am going to get my sister," Annie responded firmly.

"We got to go back and tell Fox what we know first," Bessie said. "You come now, child; we got to go back to the church."

"I can help," came a voice from the bushes. "I can help get those chi'ren back."

All of them turned to see Isaac standing at the edge of the road.

"Sweet Jesus," said Bessie, "how much worse can this get. First Annie, now you."

One of the men spoke up. "Fox ain't a violent man Isaac, but if he gets his hands on you and knows you had something to do with taking those chi'ren, he gonna kill you, sure as I am standing on this road."

"Wasn't never supposed to be like that, George. Them kids wasn't never supposed to be taken. Them kids Alden takes ain't like

Fox's kids; they needs homes. Folks is dying, ain't enough food, ain't no place to stay." He regarded at Annie with regret.

"Fox's chi'ren and kinfolk ain't never been hungry." And like the song says, 'afore I'll be a slave, I'll be buried in my grave.' Don't nobody wanna go back to that Isaac."

"I's trying to tell you, George, I didn't know they were gonna take Fox's kids. I swear."

"They shouldna took nobody's kids," Nunn shouted.

"Stop," yelled Bessie. "We ain't got time to stand here while y'all fuss. If we gonna get those chi'ren back, we got to go."

"It ain't that easy. You can't just walk on AJ's property and snatch them, kids. 'Sides that, there's been trouble over in Macon, and the Klan is riding tonight. White folks don't like General Lewis letting all the colored folks register to vote. I know Fox and a bunch of men-folk registered here in Crawford County today. I 'speck white folks know it too. Don't know if the Macon trouble gonna spill over to here. Whenever y'all go to get them kids, you gonna need a look-out; someone who can go to that barn without trouble and signal you when it's safe to get the kids." Can't nobody do that but me."

"You need to go back to the church with us and talk to Fox and Jefferson," said George.

"No, I gotta meet y'all someplace. Don't nobody up in that church wanna see me or have anything to do with me."

Bessie gazed at Isaac and slowly exhaled. "It's time for healing now, Isaac, and forgiveness amongst our people and freedom within ourselves, cause all of us ain't really free yet. I thought I was free til I walked up on Jenny James' porch and come to realize I was still scared of that woman. But then, when I peered deep in her eyes and told her what I needed, I didn't hold my head down. And even though she wasn't willing to tell me at first what I wanted to know, we both realized that she was the lesser woman for what she held back no matter what she tried to tell herself; and at that moment, I knew I was free."

"And the fault ain't all yours, Isaac. Ain't nobody ever spoke up for you. I stopped and watched AJ beat you and Alden that day by the Nickajack Creek, and I didn't even tell my mamma. Wasn't nobody around to dry your tears when AJ threatened to sell you.

Time for all of us to think about and decide what freedom is going to look like for us and to help one another get it. My mamma always said if our bodies was freed, but our minds were still in chains, well then, we wouldn't be free at all. Your mind ain't free, Isaac. Alden still owns you. But tonight, you took a big step following us and offering to help. And you bout to take an even bigger step when you walk in that church and bind yourself to your own people. Time for the Pharaoh inside each of us to let the people go."

The Rescue

As far as anyone knew, Isaac had never done an honorable thing in his life. No one trusted him, and everyone presumed he would have betrayed his own mamma had she lived, and it suited his purpose. From the time he was a sprouting boy, he connived and lied to get ahead and to save his own skin. Now, he was professing to turn over a new leaf. People had long memories, and it would be difficult for them to forget, let alone forgive. The fact was, even Isaac didn't believe in his own value and doubted if anyone would think he was sincere. He was ashamed of his past and for what happened today to those little girls.

There had been times he'd tried to do the right thing; it just never turned out right. Isaac wasn't sure Fox would understand his desire to make amends or even accept his offer to help, but he had to try.

George and Nunn led the way back to the church, with Isaac, Bessie, and Annie close behind. Clouds gathered overhead, and a raven flew above, finally landing on a hollowed-out tree stump. It sent a shudder through Isaac. *Lord Jesus, that there is a bad sign*, he thought. Bessie touched his arm as he paused and stared mournfully at the raven.

"Smells like rain, don't it, Isaac?"

He gazed at Bessie, shrugged his shoulders, and nodded. Grateful for her kindness, he tried again to apologize and explain his role in rounding up stray children, as he put it.

Nunn snapped around, eyes blazing, and glared at Isaac with contempt. He moved so close to him their noses almost touched.

"You need to shut yo mouth, Isaac. You don't care 'bout helping no chi'ren. Who was you helping back while you was riding with them patterrollers? My brother tried to run back then. You remember my brother JoJo don't you; and what they did to him after they caught him? Everybody knows you was the one who told Alden about their plans for that night? Remember them dragging him down the road in chains, stopping to whip him along the way, so's everyone would see and know what happens if you run from the master? Them owners made all the slaves round Crawford County line the road so's they could see. The dirt and the bugs filling the slashes on his back, giving him the fever for days. You remember seeing my mamma groveling in the dirt, begging for his life, don't you? They'd of cut off his leg if they didn't need him to keep on working the fields. Didn't matter too much, no way. His head banged on the ground so much; he wasn't never right no more. What? You want folk to believe you done found Jesus all of a sudden?"

Nunn spat on the ground near Isaac's feet.

Annie watched and listened, taking in the whole conversation. Nothing she had ever read, nothing her mother had ever written, described so vividly the pain and anger she heard in Nunn's voice.

"Help cometh from the Lord, Nunn, and it ain't up to us to question how he sends that help," said Bessie.

"Evil comes from the devil Bessie, and that there niggra is the devil."

"We need to keep movin,'" growled George.

They arrived at the church to find the women gone. Fox and a bunch of men waited anxiously.

Fox immediately focused on Annie and spoke to her sternly. "I figured you went following after Bessie, but you should'na done that. This ain't where you from, Missy. This here place is mighty dangerous, and you trying to take matters into your own hands don't help none."

Annie was quick to respond. "She's my sister, and she needs me. Wherever she is, she's afraid, and I want to be there when you find her. She doesn't know you. She doesn't know any of you."

Fox softened. "Annie baby, I know you think you can help, but you are going to have to trust us."

Noticing Isaac hanging back, he turned at George and Nunn. "What's Isaac doing here?"

"We know where the girls are, and we gonna need his help to rescue them."

Nunn spoke up. "You can't believe nothin' he says, Fox. If his lips is moving, you can bet he's lying. We don't need none of his help. We just need to keep him here, so he don't go warning AJ and Alden that we's coming."

"That's Fox's call to make," said Bessie emphatically.

Fox walked up to Isaac and extended his hand. "Thank you, Isaac. I 'ppreciate your offer. What you think we should do?"

Isaac cleared his throat. "I saw them chi'ren when the boys first brought them to Alden, but I wasn't sure where they took em till Miss Jenny told Bessie they was in AJ's old barn. Alden don't always keep em at the same place, and he knew I thought he should bring those two back. He's worried that they can identify him, but he ain't gonna move these ones til tomorrow, maybe the next day. I ain't sure he got a buyer as yet, but he's antsy to get em way from here. That's cause one of em is yours. He don't take kids who gots family, and important friends," he added, stealing a glance at Jefferson Long and General Lewis.

"How'd you know Bessie went to see Miss Jenny?" asked Nunn.

Isaac looked at Nunn, "I was listening outside the church. I followed you and George when you followed Bessie. Anyways, I overheard Aldean talking to his daddy. There's trouble over in Macon, and the Klan is riding tonight. I figure there will be some time when Alden and his boys is gone over yonder. I can go out to the barn and give you a signal to let you know it's safe to go in and get the kids."

Jefferson Long spoke up. "Bessie, was anyone at home with Miss Jenny when you went there?"

"Not as I could tell," she answered, watching Isaac. "Just her and the kids."

"Why you asking?" followed Fox.

"After this goes down, Alden will want someone to blame, someone to pay. He will need to send a message that people can't simply interfere with his business and take what he sees as his property."

"Jenny's oldest boy Jacob was there. He's young, but he's a talker. He could tell his daddy I was there," said Bessie.

"Alden isn't going to suspect his wife." continued Long. "She doesn't have a dog in this fight. Even if he did suspect her, he wouldn't do her any harm. But our actions are going to come back on Isaac."

Jefferson looked directly at Isaac. "Isaac, you need to understand what is about to happen. Crawford County is the only home you have ever known, but if we all come out of this alive, you will have to leave here to be safe."

Isaac exhaled and answered with sober resignation. "Ain't nothing here for me, Jefferson. I got some money saved up. Just as well that I leave. Merely got to figure out where I'll go."

"If that's what you want, I think I can be of assistance," offered General Lewis. "But you will have to leave tonight once this is done."

"Now, let's finalize this rescue plan," said Jefferson.

"What about Clara?" asked Bessie.

"Clara has always found a way to take care of Clara. She'll be fine," answered Isaac.

They finished the preparations for the rescue mission and decided who would go and who would be responsible for each phase of the plan. Satisfied with their arrangements, the men separated. Those designated to be part of the rescue agreed to a meeting point about half a mile from AJ's property. Over her objections, Fox took Bessie back to his house. She decided to go after he convinced her Mary could use the company and help with the kids. He did not let on how concerned he was for her safety.

Fox also didn't put it past Annie to try and follow them to AJ's place and thought Bessie could keep a close eye on her while Mary handled the other children. *That child is thinking with a twenty-first-century mind that don't work here*, he thought. But he had to admit, she had come up with a pretty smart idea as they were walking back to the cabin. He told Mary what Annie had suggested, and she got right on it.

As he left the cabin, he turned to Bessie and said, "If something goes wrong, you have to be able to tell the army folks and the people from the Freedmen's Bureau who's responsible. They may not care much about what happens to a bunch of us colored folks, but they will care if something happens to General Lewis."

The cloud cover blocked out the moon as Isaac made his way to the dilapidated barn. AJ no longer farmed, and the few animals he kept were in pens on the other side of the field. Isaac crept up to the barn, determined to make sure the girls were still there before going back to meet up with Fox and the others. He needed to be sure Alden hadn't moved the kids without his knowledge. If that happened, and the kids weren't there when Fox and the others arrived, no one would ever believe his intentions had been above board.

"What you doing sneaking round here, boy?"

Isaac jumped at the sound of AJ's deep-throated voice, still strong despite the toll taken by war, tobacco, and hard living. Seconds passed before Isaac spoke. He hadn't thought of what he would say if caught since he assumed if anyone came, it would be Alden, and his suspicions could be easily dampened. Running into AJ was unforeseen and frightening.

"Evenin' Mr. AJ. I knowed Alden was gonna be busy this evenin', and I thought I would check up on his merchandise to make sure everything was ok."

"That so," AJ said suspiciously. "Why wouldn't everything be OK?"

"I hear one of them kids is known to Jefferson Long, and with him being a politician and all, I thought I would check."

The sound of thundering hooves jolted both men as ghostly figures on horseback in white robes with hoods covering their heads and carrying torches came through the trees. One spoke directly to AJ.

"Sir, I do apologize for coming up on you unexpectedly, but we have been searching for a colored boy for a few hours now, and I believe this might be the one. He stole some livestock from over at the Calhoun place."

"I ain't stole nothin'" cried Isaac. "Tell 'em, Mr. AJ. I may be a lot of things, but I ain't no thief."

AJ laughed. "You a niggra ain't you? Is that what you was up to Isaac, thinking you was gonna hide from these gentlemen in my old barn?"

Another man reached for the rope hanging from the side of his saddle and began forming a noose. The first man spoke again.

"Sir, I think it might be best, given you are not attired for this evening's festivities, that you head back to your home and take refuge with your wife. We are not the only ones out riding this evening. With trouble over in Macon and coloreds like this one taking the liberty of so many menfolk being over there, the Yankee Army is riding as well. We would not want you to be recognized, should they happen upon us this fine evening. We, on the other hand, will be riding quite hard after we take care of this boy. We will move off your property in a timely fashion."

The other man pitched the rope over a tree branch.

"Mr. AJ please," begged Isaac.

"Always knew you'd end up hanging from a tree, Isaac." AJ threw his head back and laughed as two men grabbed Isaac and dragged him towards the tree.

"We can take care of this here or a bit away from your property, sir. What is your pleasure?"

"Ha, I don't care where you carry him."

Once AJ was out of sight, General John Lewis pulled off his hood and whispered loudly, "hurry up."

Fox, who had held back near the trees, yanked the hood from his head and ran to the barn.

"Damn, you boys scared the life outta me," said Isaac. Where'd y'all get them sheets?" he went on while running after Fox.

"Old sly Fox always gotta backup plan," murmured Fox.

"Why was you here instead of the meeting place, Isaac?" asked Nunn.

"Enough," whispered Jefferson, we need to get those girls and get out of here now."

They entered the barn and found Emma and Mary Jane tied to a post. "I knew you'd find us," shouted Emma.

Fox put his finger to his lips. "We got to hurry, baby. Mary Jane, you ride with me, Emma; you go with Mr. Long."

"Papa," said Mary Jane haltingly. He tilted his head and realized she was pointing to two children tied up on the other side of the barn.

"Oh no," groaned Nunn. "We can't take them. We got to go."

"I ain't leaving them, "said Fox. "I'll take one," said Lewis, "I got the other," said Isaac.

"Nunn, you and George ride straight home. Blow out the candles and get everyone in the bed. We don't want Alden to blame any more people than he can prove."

"I mentioned Jefferson's name to AJ. I didn't mean to," said Isaac.

"Don't worry about that," said Jefferson. We'll work on that later. Get going."

They rode as fast as they could back to Fox's cabin. The rain Bessie predicted earlier started to fall. It was heavy but not destined to last long. It turned out to be a good thing because it washed away the tracks made by their horses.

They soon made it home and rushed into the cabin with the four children. The commotion in the small cabin bordered on chaos. Mary fell to her knees as Annie threw herself at Emma. The two other children held back, but Mary reached for them and hugged them as well.

"Alright now," said Lewis, "you all need to settle down a bit," but he was smiling from ear to ear.

Fox grinned back. "Didn't know you could sound like such a Georgia gentleman General."

"Didn't realize you could pull off pretending to be a member of the Klan," Lewis laughed.

Fox glanced over at Annie. "That was a real smart idea you had about having those sheets and pretending to be Klansmen. Don't know what Mary's gonna do 'bout replacing those sheets she laundered for them ladies," he laughed.

Mary hugged Mary Jane again and then went to Isaac. "Thank you, Isaac, thank you for bringing my baby back to me."

Isaac sheepishly bobbed his head.

Mary fixed a light meal while George Lewis slipped out to make plans. He returned shortly with a wagon and spoke directly to Isaac.

"Isaac, do you have your things?"

"Yes, sir. I gathered them before I went over to AJ's place."

Lewis went on to tell the group his plans for Isaac and the children that had been rescued from the barn.

"I spoke to these children before I left, and, as we suspected, they are orphans, turned out after the war ended. I am taking them with us. They need to be as far away from Alden and his men as we can get them. I've got my wagon in the back. We will ride over to Knoxville and meet up with some people I know. Isaac, they will get you farther up north. I have contacts in Virginia and Washington DC who will assist you and take the children."

Bessie spoke up. "I'm going with Isaac. I can help with the children."

Fox, Mary, and General Lewis spoke up at once, but Bessie held up her hand, taking command of the dimly lit room.

"My leaving makes sense, especially with these here kids. God knows Isaac wouldn't know what to do with two scared children for hundreds of miles. Besides, you can make Alden think me and Isaac plotted it out for me and him to take all the children and trade 'em for something. Colored folks is trying to make money to get resettled. Alden knows Isaac, and I go way back. Annie here says she got to get Emma home, so I'm guessing they won't be here when the sun comes up."

She raised her eyebrows to Fox as if seeking confirmation. He nodded his head in return.

"You should put out the word that Annie and Josh went for a walk with me and never came back. Then say late in the night, someone dropped Mary Jane off here at home, and she told y'all Isaac, and I left with the three kids visiting Mary and Fox, along with two other children y'all didn't know. You spread that around so's Clara hears it and sho nuff it will get back to Alden. 'Sides," she said, winking at Mary, "Clara will be right miffed thinking Isaac done run off with me."

As for me leaving, well, my mamma is gone, and truth to it, Isaac and I come up together. He's the closest thing I got to family. Somebody needs to take care of this fool."

Isaac grinned at Bessie and blushed. She slowly blew out a breath. "General Lewis, I testify I can be of good help up North. I can sew and weave, and I can read and write."

Astonished, everyone stared at Bessie. "Jenny taught me a long time ago, and I've been practicing and getting better over the years."

General Lewis bowed slightly to Bessie. "If you want to leave, Bessie, you're welcome to come along."

"Thank you, sir."

Hugs went all around, and Bessie told Mary she might come back one day, but both women knew that was just talk.

Isaac, General Lewis, and the children went out of the door, but Bessie held back for just a moment.

"Fox, I would like to ask a favor of you.

Please tell Nunn that Isaac didn't tell Alden about his brother JoJo's plan to run, though he does blame himself for what happened to him.

All the while Jenny was teaching me to read and write, I was teaching Isaac.

Isaac wrote the pass that JoJo had on him the night the patterrollers caught him. Isaac didn't know Alden would be riding that night. If he hadn't been, JoJo might have got away on that pass, but Alden saw JoJo and knew he had no business being where he was. He figured out the pass was fake. Isaac always said if he hadn't written that pass, JoJo might never have tried to run and got beat so badly."

Bessie turned and walked out of the McElmurry cabin and away from Crawford County. Annie Sesstry learned yet another lesson from the day's adventure.

Going Home

Fox stepped out into the steamy night. The rain showers that passed through earlier had done little to cool things off. Rocking back on his heels and rubbing his neck, he gazed skyward, resigned to the fact that tomorrow they would have to deal with Alden. But for tonight, the girls were safe, Isaac and Bessie were on their way to a new life, and lo and behold, he had registered to vote. Walked right up to that woman and registered. *Free men register*, he thought. *Free men vote, and by God, I am a free man.* The corners of his mouth turned up with satisfaction.

He watched the fireflies winking through the woods, and his thoughts drifted to the unknown ancestors, his and all the other restless spirits who defied time and space to beckon their descendants through the ages and plead to be found. He knew they would not rest until that day. These children, these Travelers, were not Fox's first visitors. They would not be his last. His visitors were not often from his family, but that didn't matter. All the Unknowns shared a common desire to reclaim their identity. They all deserved justice and dignity, and he would do his part. Through some ordinance of God, they sent their descendants on a pilgrimage through time to restore their stolen past. They sent them to anyone who could help close the circle and make them whole. But this time had been extraordinary. He had been allowed to see his legacy in these children and what a legacy it was.

He was mystified at having three come at once this time, especially two as young as Emma and Josh. That had never happened before, and none had ever stayed a full day, just a few moments in time, an hour at most. What did this mean?

"Lordy," he mumbled aloud, "trying to figure out who's who over two hundred years just don't seem possible. But neither does moving through time."

Fox didn't hear Annie come outside. She slipped behind him and touched his arm. He turned and smiled.

"Thank you for saving Emma. I'm sorry about Mary Jane. I don't think she would have gone berry-picking if she hadn't had Emma for company. Emma didn't know it wasn't safe."

"Don't go playing what-ifs," he chided mildly.

"What if they hadn't gone? What if they went this way and not that way?"

"When people do bad things, we can't pardon them even a little bit by thinking we the ones who did something wrong. Emma and Mary Jane had every right to go berry-picking without fear of being taken. Just like the Unknowns had a right to be doing whatever they was doing in their country without fear of being stolen and sold. God gives us those rights, Annie, and when a man or a woman takes them away, the fault lies with the people doing the taking. I believe that with all my heart. I think that's why one of our Unknown Ancestors picked me to be a part of all this, and they picked you too."

"You got to believe in what's right and speak up. I know that's hard, and sometimes I don't know if I'm always up to it. I don't know if anyone is up to it, and I speck some who have traveled like you have gone back to their times and rejected the call. I hope you don't do that. No matter what happens, we have to keep trying. You are one special young lady, and I think there are great things ahead for you. I think that drawing you do is going to make you famous one day."

Annie smiled as she thought about Fox's words. "In my time, they have something called DNA testing. They use your blood or spit to tell where your ancestors came from. My Aunt Lizzy, Josh's mom, did the test, and it turns out our ancestors, yours and mine, came from Cameroon in West Africa. They were from the Bamileke tribe.

I did a Black History Month school report on the Bamileke clans because so many enslaved people came from Cameroon.

The Bamileke people trace their origins to Egypt, and some believe they are descendants of kings and queens. They were strong and virile and highly sought after during the slave trade. There were many clans among the Bamileke, most of them with their kings and chiefs, and they were often at war with one another. Some of their leaders may have sold them to slave traders as punishment for crimes or because of rivalries among the clans. White and black men stole some of them; others were tricked into going onto the slave ships."

Fox's forehead furrowed. "What in kingdom come is Black History Month."

Annie laughed at the expression on Fox's face. She laughed with an abandon she hadn't felt in a long time. With laughter came the release of the tension of the day. Despite all the trauma, she was happy, happier than she had been in a while. *This is the most fantastic thing ever*, she thought. I'm a Traveler. *The Unknown picked me!*

Thinking about that, she mustered the courage to speak openly. As Fox had said, *believe in what's right and speak up.*

"I believe the Unknowns want to use the Travelers to send messages backward as well as forward in time, and I would like for you to think about something. Your Ann should go to school. She should learn to read and write, just like Bessie did. It's not too late, and girls need education as much as boys do. They need to be able to do more than cook and take care of babies. And boys can help with that stuff too. Reading makes everything possible. All the children should go to school. Education is power. Just like registering and voting is power and knowing where you came from is power."

Fox looked at her for a moment before responding. "I'll see to it."

He put his arm around her and walked her inside.

They entered the four-room house as everyone was preparing for bed. Annie walked over to Emma and Josh, pulled them close to her, and kissed them.

"Ewe," said Josh. "Don't get all mushy. Did you find out how we get home? This has been interesting, but I've had enough."

"Me too," said Emma.

Annie giggled. "It won't be long."

Her eyes circled the room, and she knew she would one day draw this scene, though not right now. The sight would be etched in her mind forever, and she would take her time later to capture every detail. The long plank table and simple benches, the chair in one corner, the fireplace for cooking in the other. The rack with hooks that hung over it and pots dangling from the hooks. There was a bed in the room where the boys slept horizontally. There were two other rooms, one with two beds for the girls, who, like the boys, slept horizontally. The other was for Fox and Mary. None of them had doors. The mattresses laid out on the large platform beds were swaths of fabric stuffed with straw. In the winter, she had learned, the straw would be exchanged for cotton. It was so different from her home, but home, filled with love and laughter, built by Fox's hands. She would draw it for Fox's descendants, for her children and grandchildren.

Mary went to Annie and gave her a big hug. She told the children to give Annie, Emma, and Josh a hug and to say goodbye because they would be gone by morning.

"Where y'all going?" asked Henry

"Time for them to go back home now," said Mary.

"How they gonna get there?"

"Don't ask so many questions," said Fox.

"Can they stay for a story?"

"I reckon," said Fox with a smile.

Fox pulled up the one chair in the large room and called the children to sit around him.

"I want the bird story," said Amos.

"Then the bird story is what it will be," answered Fox.

As he started, he nodded at Annie, arched an eyebrow, and winked. She knew it was time.

Fox's melodious voice began.

"There was once a beautiful bird who grew up proud and happy in her village. She had lots of family and lots of fellow birds who loved her. As she got to be grown, she decided she wanted to leave the village and seek her way in the big world," he glanced at Annie and chuckled, "'cause she could read and write. Things started out fine, but as she made her way on the journey, she met a flock of mean old birds who aggrieved her and called her names; said she didn't need to go on no journey since she wasn't never gonna mount to nothin' no way. She tried to keep going, but them birds kept at her, saying she wasn't smart, she didn't look like much, and she had skinny little bird legs that wouldn't take her far. Those mean birds made the village bird doubt herself so much; she forgot all she had learned. She got so afraid she couldn't keep going forward towards her dreams. She turned around and flew back to the village.

When she got there, her friends and family asked her what happened, and she told them about those mean old birds. Her Papa bird and the others reminded her of how special she was, told her 'bout all the gifts God had given her. Told her it would be a downright sin and a shame to waste those gifts because of some silly old mean birds. She hugged her Papa bird and thanked everyone, and headed out again, bold and full of courage. As she was leaving, she bent down and, with her beak, picked up a stone to hold on to, to remind herself of the village, those she loved, and those who loved her. She turned and took one last look back, and went on her way.

When she saw those mean old birds again, she didn't pay them no mind. She knew where she come from and where she was headed. That little bird went on to do great things.

Some years later she went back to her village for a visit and was surprised to see a statue there that looked just like her. The statue's feet was going forward, but its head was turned around looking back, and it had a stone in its beak. The chief bird saw her staring up at the statue and explained that the statue had been placed in the center of the village after she left the second time so all the other young birds in the village would know of her journey and the lessons she had learned. They would know it was important for them to look back and understand where they came from, to move forward toward who and what they were meant to be.

They would be reminded because she had once forgotten. The chief walked her to the other side, so she could see that her name had been carved on the statue. When the young birds were in doubt, they would call out her name, which would forever have the power to guide and lead them on the right path."

Annie contemplated her surroundings and, through tears, she could see all the children, including Josh and Emma, had fallen asleep. Then she gazed back at her great-great-great-great-grandfather.

"Do you know what name was carved on that statue, Annie?" Fox asked.

She looked at Fox one final time, closed her eyes, and whispered, "Sankofa."

And the Truth Will Set You Free

Before she opened her eyes, Annie recognized the familiar sounds and smells of her own time. Comforted by the sharpness of her senses, she knew she was no longer in 1867. The tip of her nose tickled with the aroma of coffee nearby. Her ears prickled with the sound of a honking car, and the air breaks of a bus were alien to Crawford County and 1867. A jarring tangle of voices assaulted her brain, sending a piercing pain to her head. She reached her hand up to rub her temple as she opened her eyes.

She was lying on the ground with her head in her mother's lap. Her father was off to the side on his cell phone. Emma and Josh were standing over her, their tense faces drawn with concern. Despite her numbing headache, she smiled at them. "We're back, guys."

"We?" questioned Josh mockingly.

"Back from where?" challenged Emma.

Annie sat up and looked suspiciously at her sister and cousin. "Back from Georgia. Back from 1867, which should be hard to forget."

Emma giggled. "Wow, you got hit harder than I thought."

"What's that supposed to mean? Don't act as if we didn't have the most amazing experience of a lifetime."

Blinking at Emma and Josh's apparent confusion, Annie drilled. "You do know what happened to us and where we've been, don't you?"

"I know what happened to you," said Josh.

"We were standing here about to take a picture, and out of nowhere, a ball flew up and hit you in the head. It knocked you out cold."

John walked over and bent down to examine Annie. "How are you doing, kiddo?"

"I'm fine, dad, but something is wrong with Emma and Josh."

"I don't believe we need to take her to the hospital," he said to Sophie. "But we'll keep an eye on her. Lizzy can take a check her out when she gets home. Your mother will be here in a few minutes. She's going to drive you and Ann to the house. I'll take Josh and Emma on the metro and pick up the car."

Annie cocked her head to one side and fixed her eyes on Josh. "You really don't remember anything that happened?"

John reached down to help Annie as she steadied herself to stand. But she moved quicker than he anticipated. She jumped up and closed in on Josh. Breathing heavily in his face, repeating her question.

"You don't remember anything that happened?"

Josh didn't respond, and Annie became more agitated and combative.

"Why did Jim Barrie write the story of Peter Pan, Josh? Who was Peter Pan to him?"

Confused and intimidated, Josh took a step back from Annie.

"Answer me, Josh," Annie pursued.

He blinked and slowly replied, "Barrie's brother died when they were kids. Peter Pan represented his brother, the boy who never grew up."

Triumphantly Annie pushed on, poking Josh in the chest.

"Ha. Where did you learn that Josh, when did you learn it?"

"I don't know. I guess I read it."

"No, you didn't read it," Annie hissed, "Mamie told you that. Our great-great-grandmother told you that."

Josh was on the verge of tears. He didn't want to upset Annie, but her banter was scary, and it was getting to him.

"That's enough, Ann," her mother declared. "We're leaving. Gramby will be here soon. John, you head to the metro with Josh and Emma. We'll see you at home."

"Why can't we take the metro?" asked Annie.

"Because I want to get you home," answered her mother.

Sophie and Annie walked toward the monument drop-off lot.

"Mom, I know it sounds crazy, but Emma, Josh, and I went back in time, and we met a ton of our ancestors. We met Mamie Calhoun, Gramby's grandmother."

"I know who Mamie Calhoun was. She was my great-grandmother," said Sophie, "and she wasn't around in 1867."

"I know," moaned Annie. "We made a stop before we went to 1867. It's complicated."

"It does sound crazy. But I am going to give you a pass for now because you got hit on the head hard enough to get knocked out. But I swear, Ann, if you keep talking like this, if you keep hassling Josh, I am going to take your phone and ground you."

"But how would I know about Peter Pan? How would Josh?"

"For goodness sakes, Ann. Peter Pan has been Josh's favorite story since he was three years old. I'm sure he read the history of the characters someplace or heard about it. Regardless, it doesn't give you the right to jump on his case as you did. Now I am done talking about this." Annie fell into a sullen silence and made no more attempts to talk to her mother.

Sophie's mother, Rose, was at the parking area when they approached. The tension between her daughter and granddaughter was evident, and Rose did her best to ignore it.

"How are my girls today? You took a good one upside your head, Annie. I can see a knot. I figured that might happen and brought an ice pack for you to put on it."

Tears were already forming in Annie's eyes. *Could it all have been a crazy dream? Not possible,* she argued with herself. *There's too much detail, too much information. It's seared in my memory forever. Besides, if everyone is right, I wasn't out long enough to have a dream with that much detail. The Unknown made this happen. He or she also made Emma and Josh forget.*

Rose watched at her daughter before pulling away from the curb.

"So, this sounds like it's been an eventful morning. Did you call Lizzy, so she can come straight home and examine Annie?"

Lost in her thoughts Sophie, responded with a slight shake of her head. She noticed her mother's disapproving expression and added. "John said you were going to call her."

"That's not how the conversation went," groused Rose.

She headed to Great Falls, driving along Canal Road, crossing the Chain Bridge. She covertly stole glances at her granddaughter in the rearview mirror as she drove. She tried to get Sophie and Ann to talk, but each stared out of the window, lost in her own thoughts. "OK," she uttered with exasperation, "what's up with you two?"

"Ann had some daydream when she was out, and Josh and Emma were in the dream."

"It wasn't a dream," mumbled Annie.

"She was very rude to Josh when he tried to point out to her that he and Emma didn't have a clue about her dream and that whatever she was talking about wasn't real."

Rose looked in the mirror at her granddaughter.

"What kind of dream?"

"She says they time-traveled."

"She didn't ask you," snapped Annie.

Sophie wheeled around in the seat. "Have you lost your mind? You do not speak to me that way."

"I don't have to speak to you at all. You'll only believe what Josh or Emma say anyway."

Annie's words stung and stunned Sophie. Her daughter had never answered her back.

Rose intervened before things deteriorated further.

"Let's get Ann home, let her lay down. We can talk after everyone calms down."

Rose pulled up to the Sesstry house and had barely stopped the car before Annie jumped out. She had to wait for her mother to unlock the door, but as soon as it was opened, she bolted up the stairs to her room and slammed the door. She threw herself on her bed and cried until she fell asleep.

Annie wasn't sure how long she slept, but when she woke up, she went into the bathroom to rinse the pasty taste from her mouth. Washing her hands, she scraped over the splinter in her finger. She stared slack-jawed at the piece of wood that had traveled with her through time. The splintered triggered something else. She had forgotten all about the pictures she had drawn throughout the day. They hadn't been able to bring the plastic bottles and the telephone with them back in time, but the sketchbook traveled with her there, and she was sure it had returned. She needed her backpack. Now. She could prove they had traveled through time with the sketchbook.

She rushed out of the bathroom and found her grandmother standing in her room.

"I knocked, but there was no answer. I wanted to make sure you were feeling alright."

"Gramby, it wasn't a dream, and I can prove it."

Her grandmother ignored her comment and moved to her bed, and sat down. She patted the spot next to her in a motion signifying she wanted Annie to take a seat. Knowing better than to argue, Annie slumped and sat beside Rose.

"Did I ever tell you about the camp we went to as kids? Camp Minisink. It was where all the cool kids in New Your City went during the summer."

Oh God, thought Annie, one of Gramby's stories, and somehow the Good Lord is probably going to have a part in it to teach me a lesson about today. But I can prove it happened if she would let me.

Her grandmother went on. "At Camp Minisink, there was this old, dilapidated cabin in the hills; Peter Quick's Cabin. There were dozens of ghost stories about that cabin dating back to the 1800s. Most of them had to do with Peter Quick's wife and how she died. The kind of stories kids make up that change and morph with each passing summer. Some said her husband killed her, and you could see traces of her blood on the rocks near the cabin. Another tail was that Indians scalped Peter Quick and abducted his wife. That one figured the so-called blood outside the cabin was his, not hers. For the life of me, I don't know why we knew his name and not hers.

Please stop talking, thought Annie.

"Anyway, one day during the summer after I turned thirteen, I was at camp and went walking alone in the hills and went to Peter Quick's cabin. I saw this girl standing there and thought it was the ghost of Peter Quick's wife."

Frustrated by Rose's rambling, Annie attempted to interrupt her grandmother to tell her about her sketchbook, but Rose held up her hand to stop Annie from speaking.

"As I was saying, when I saw that ghost, I was terrified. I ran as fast as my feet would carry me away from there, and I didn't tell a soul what I had seen. I knew everyone would laugh at me or think I was trying to make up a new tale. I guess I felt a lot like you did when you woke up after you were hit in the head, and Josh, Emma, and your mother didn't believe you.

Here it comes, thought Annie.

"Well, for two or three days, I could think of nothing else but that girl. I realized it couldn't have been Mrs. Quick because she was supposed to be white, and the girl I had seen was Black and too young to be anyone's wife. Well, you know me. I wasn't going to rest until I figured out who or what I had seen. So, I scrounged up the courage to go back to the cabin; and would you believe it, I peeked in and standing there in that cabin with all the holes in the roof and signs of the animals who came and went, was this Black girl about fifteen or sixteen years old. She wore a long black skirt, a white blouse, a necktie, and a straw hat. She didn't appear to be a ghost, but she didn't look like she was from 1962 either. She didn't say a word, but she held out her hand to me, and I stepped in and took it."

Rose finally had Annie's attention.

"In an instant, that girl and I were transformed to another time and place. She and I were standing on a red clay country road, and she invited me to take a walk with her. We started to stroll down that dusty road just like it was a normal kind of day. She asked me if I knew who my people were. I started to name my parents, but she stopped me and asked if I knew who my ancestors were. I stared at her. Then she told me of the story of the Unknowns, the millions of Africans brought to this country during the slave trade who had their identities stripped from them. She said their spirits wander through time in a quest to have their identities unveiled by their descendants. She told me I was a Traveler, and there was at least one and there would continue to be at least one in every generation until the end of time. It was the Travelers' responsibility to help the Unknowns, to gather information about them so that one day they would be no longer be anonymous. I have a suspicion this sounds a bit familiar to you. Am I right?"

A stunned Annie nodded her head at Rose.

I asked the girl how the information was shared across generations. She said family members were griots, or storytellers in one way or another, some through song, some through stories, some through art, and that one day, Travelers would start to find each other, and the quest would be strengthened.

"After we had walked a while, the girl pointed to a slight hill and told me to go to the top and look down. I did as I was told, but before I looked down, I glanced back to see if she was still with me, but she was gone. I turned and gazed in the direction she'd pointed to, and I saw her sitting under a tree reading a book. I heard a voice say, that's Mamie. She's going to college this fall, the first one in our family. I couldn't take my eyes off the young girl who bore the same name as my grandmother.

"Three children approached her. I didn't know who they were, and I couldn't hear what they were saying. I saw Mamie give them something to drink from a canteen. They talked awhile, especially Mamie and the boy. Then they were watching at a flash of light and got excited and gathered their things. They hugged Mamie and ran to the end of a grove of trees. They held hands, counted to three, and I heard them yell, Sankofa."

"I woke up on the ground. Annie, I've never told this story to anyone. I wanted to, but I was afraid no one would believe me. As I grew older, the story faded from memory, and I convinced myself it had been a dream that never happened. As a teacher, I made sure I told stories of enslaved people, some famous, but most that I learned about through research. I gave my students projects that required them to learn something about their ancestors.

I never heard a story in my family about any Travelers. As far as I know, no one ever admitted being a Traveler. We always honored our Unknown Ancestors at family reunions, but I don't know how the practice started.

I sometimes thought my Aunt Nell might be a Traveler, but she never said a word about it, and I was afraid to ask. I was waiting for a sign from the Unknown, a sign that never came until today.

I never thought much about those children. My memory was always of Mamie; That is until today when your mother mentioned your so-called daydream. While you were asleep, Josh and Emma came home. I remembered Emma's outfit as soon as I saw her," she half-laughed, "and I realized I saw the three of you over fifty years ago visit with my grandmother when I traveled through time."

Annie could not believe what she was hearing.

"You traveled through time and saw us meet your grandmother Mamie when you were thirteen. But she wasn't the only one we met. After you saw us, we went farther back in time where we met Fox and Mary McElmurry and most of their children. Their Emma hadn't been born yet. I think stopping to see Mamie was a gesture from the Unknown for Josh. He connected with her and whatever she said to him gave him some peace about the loss of uncle Darryl. She convinced him that love and family never end."

"The thing is, Fox said Emma and Josh being there may have been a mistake, that they were too young. Now they don't even remember going," Annie said dejectedly. "I guess you have to be thirteen."

"I don't believe the Unknowns make mistakes," said Rose. "The rules may be changing. You went to two different periods in time, and you met a lot of people. You stayed a long time, and Josh and Emma were there for a reason. The tactics of the Unknows may be taking a new direction. You know, we are coming up on four hundred years since slavery began in this country. The Israelites were in slavery in Egypt for four hundred years until the Good Lord sent Moses."

"So, Mamie was a Traveler; maybe Aunt Nell was too. Then you and now me, but you don't know who was between you and me."

"No idea. I suspect it's one of my cousin's kids. It doesn't have to follow directly down the line, and I'm not even sure about Aunt Nell. I know it's a person who descended from the Unknown and most likely from Fox and Mary."

"I wonder who it could be," mused Annie.

"I think that would be me," came a halting voice from the doorway.

A New Bond

nnie and Rose turned to see Sophie standing in the doorway, clutching Annie's sketch pad to her chest. The backpack Annie carried through time hung over her shoulder.

While Annie napped, Sophie had retrieved the backpack from the car, and the book fell out. She absently browsed through the sketchbook but was confused by what she saw. The family Sankofa sketch was there were, but so too were a series of drawings of unfamiliar people from the past. The pictures had not been there before. Annie could not have drawn them in the time it had taken her and John to visit the souvenir shop. The people in the sketches and everything about the settings were not Annie's genre. But there was no mistaking her style. Annie drew these pictures. The question was when?

She sprinted up the stairs in time to hear her mother tell her extraordinary story of time travel. Sophie knew in her heart that her daughter had indeed been to the past. Moreover, pieces of a puzzle from her early teenage years began to fall in place.

Sophie's voice caught as she asked Annie about the sketches in the book.

"Please tell me about these," she said.

"Come and sit," suggested Rose.

Bewildered, Sophie moved to her daughter's bed. She perched on the other side of Annie. She did her best to remain calm and absorb the conversation she had overheard. Folding her legs beneath her, she pushed the sketchbook into Annie's hand.

"I'm sorry about earlier," Annie said.

"I know," answered Sophie.

Annie smiled at her mother and began recounting her fantastic journey. She started with the first sighting of Mamie in the village that morning.

"Mamie has a unique connection to the Unknown and the Travelers in our line," said Annie. "She's not quite like other Travelers. She's our north star, and I felt a special connection with her from the moment I saw her in the village. When we were heading to the metro, I thought I saw her in modern-day clothes. When Gramby traveled and saw her talking to us, she was preparing us for a visit to 1867. She's like a guardian angel or talisman."

"Tell us everything that happened today," urged Sophie.

As she turned each page of the sketchbook, Annie shared her story. She showed them the sketches she did of Mamie from memory in place of Dr. King at the memorial. Then, in honey-sweet tones, she told an astonishing tale of how she, Josh, and Emma traveled through time.

She spoke of the wall, the magic in the word Sankofa in certain places. She told them how they found themselves in rural Georgia in 1912. They walked for miles before coming upon Mamie sitting under the tree. Annie theorized the encounter with Mamie in Lizella was a temporary stop to prepare them for the more exciting adventure to come. She also thought it was an intervention for Josh. Mamie understood his pain over losing his father.

"She was reading Peter Pan and Wendy. Josh's favorite story and he said he thought Mamie looked like you, Gramby. Emma and I went to the bathroom in the bushes, if you can believe it, and Mamie and Josh had some time alone together. Josh doubted her at first; then, he was intrigued by her. Finally, when we were leaving, he told her he thought she was going to be a really good teacher. He said he knew he would see his father again someday, and her too."

Rose nodded when Annie said she would like to tell Lizzy about it later.

Annie continued with her story. She told them about arriving in Crawford County near the courthouse on the day Fox registered to vote for the first time. She told them about meeting Fox, Mary, and the children and how strange it was to know they were her ancestors. Rose and Sophie marveled at the idea of Annie and the other kids going to a family picnic in 1867. Annie admitted she discovered a new appreciation for the privilege of going to school when she recalled Ann's hunger to learn to read. She commented on how far-out it was to meet historical figures like Jefferson Long and General John Lewis.

She decided not to tell her mother about the kidnapping of Emma and Mary Jane just yet. It would be a story for another day when Josh and Emma could recall their journey and Emma could tell her own story. Besides, Sophie was too unsettled to complicate the situation with the information about Klansmen taking Emma and nearly selling her into slavery.

Annie told them about going to church and the emotion she felt hearing a hymn raised in the original tradition of their people. She said she better understood now how much music meant to both the enslaved and freedmen. She ended her story by retelling Fox's version of the legend of the Sankofa at the house before right before returning to their own time. She reflected on the peacefulness of the scene of the kids listening to Fox's bedtime story, despite a day of excitement and unexpected visitors.

"They sort of roll with life's circumstances, which is totally amazing."

She promised to recreate the home scene on canvas as soon as possible.

"These sketches are drafts. I plan to do my first serious series on Crawford County Georgia and Reconstruction."

Rose ran her hand through Annie's hair. "What a talented and lucky girl you are. I could not be prouder of you."

"Nor I," said Sophie.

Rose turned to Sophie.

"I don't understand why you said you think you might be the Traveler from your generation. Either you traveled, or you didn't."

Sophie sighed and shrugged.

"I should never have questioned you. But my experience was so strange; I was sure it was my imagination. I lacked your courage to speak about it. Perhaps that's why the Unknows are taking a different approach," she laughed.

"You've heard the story of how I came to be such a ferocious reader. For my second birthday, my godfather gave me a little record player that came with several books. I could play a record and follow along with the book. It would chime when it was time to turn the page."

"She played with that thing non-stop" added Rose. "She began recognizing words, and by the time she was three, she was a full-on reader."

"This is my story, Mom," admonished Sophie.

"But she's right. I could read, and it was all I ever wanted to do. By the time I was in elementary school, I was the only kid whose parents had to make her stop reading and go outside to play. I was shy, and I not only read books, but I also became the characters in the books and got lost in the stories."

"Like Josh does," interjected Annie.

"Just like Josh does," said Sophie.

"One day, not long after I turned thirteen, I was in the library. The lights blinked, and the room went dark. When the room brightened again, I was in someone's home. Actually, it was a cabin. A girl was sitting by a fire reading. Annie, I bet you can guess what she was wearing."

"Uh, would that be a long black skirt, a white blouse, a necktie, and a straw hat?" Annie guessed.

"OK, she didn't have on the hat or the tie," said Sophie smiling, "but it was a long black skirt and a white blouse."

At first, I didn't consider it strange since I always put myself into the stories I read. But as I thought about it, this was a different experience. For one, I never entered a book as Sophia Clarkson. I became a character in the book, usually the central character, but not in this instance. I was still Sophie. Besides that, I was not dressed like the girl or her times. I had on jeans and a hockey jersey. Most of all, when the lights went out at the library, I wasn't reading a book by or about a girl in a log cabin. I thought it might be a dream, but I knew I hadn't gone to bed, and it felt too real. I never gave any consideration to the idea that I had traveled through time."

"At last, the girl, who I now know, thanks to your drawings, was our very own Mamie, spoke to me and asked if I knew who my people were. I started to name my parents, but, like your grandmother, she stopped me and asked if I knew who my ancestors were. I didn't answer. She gestured to the book she was reading and told me it was a book of poems by Phillis Wheatley, the first African American woman to ever have her works published. Phillis was taken from her homeland at the age of seven and brought to America on a slave ship named the Phillis. The people who purchased her named her after the ship that brought her to this country. Mamie told me Phillis Wheatley lost her family and her name just as our ancestors did."

"She went on to say she was going to be a teacher and teach Phillis Wheatly's poems. She said one day, someone in her family might become a writer and tell the story of her people and help restore their identities. The candles flickered, and I was back in the library with my head down on the desk. There was a book about Phillis Wheatley in the pile of books I had pulled from the shelves. I convinced myself I had fallen asleep and had a weird dream. From that day to this, I have written stories about the history of Black people coming to this land."

Annie reached for her mother and hugged her, then turned to her grandmother and did the same.

Jumping from the bed, Annie began to pace with excitement.

"Now what?" she exclaimed.

"Now nothing," said Rose. "We do what we've always done. We go on with our lives. We've traveled to the past, and we learned from it. We will always search for ways to use those lessons to teach others about our heritage; who we are, why we are, where we've come from, and what our ancestors experienced."

"You're right, mom," said Sophie. "Both of us traveled, and it shaped who we are and what we became. You met Mamie, our family's first educator, and wound up dedicating your life to the field of education, like so many others in our family. She led me to write, and my career path has focused on telling the African American story in truth and fiction. Miss Ann here was at a sculpture, a piece of art when she traveled, and now she has a vision of what she wants to do with her gift. Time travel has served its purpose."

Annie stopped moving and glared at her mother and grandmother with disbelief.

"I can't believe either of you. That's it? You got to travel back in time, meet an ancestor and choose a career. I didn't have one brief encounter with Mamie like you two. I met others, and I saw the past in a way neither of you did. No way am I done. I am traveling again and soon. And I'm not waiting and hoping for luck to give me another shot. I am going to figure out how to make it happen. Sankofa, abracadabra, Tinkerbell's fairy dust - whatever it takes to make it happen."

"Drawing pictures of one adventure will never be enough for me. The Unknowns had their hearts broken, and it's up to us to make them whole again, or to at least try. The more I travel, the better equipped I'll be able to help do that. Listening to your stories, I know it's not just a word or a place, but circumstances and a state of mind that make traveling possible. Fox met our Unknown Ancestor at the back of a barn and was taken to a slave ship. He or she told Fox that their Spirit had called Fox to him or her. None of us traveled to meet the Unknown, but the Spirit of the Unknown made our traveling possible. The spirit of our ancestor and the spirits of millions more are out there somewhere directing travelers' movements. One of them is going to guide me on another journey. And that journey is going to open up a whole new world about our family and our history."

Before Annie could go on, Emma stuck her head in the door.

"Hey, you guys, what are you doing?" Aunt Lizzy is downstairs with pizza. Annie, she wants to examine you to make sure you haven't lost your marbles."

Annie grabbed her sketchbook and Emma's hand and rushed out of the room. Turning to her mother and grandmother, she pleaded with her eyes and finally spoke.

"Mom, Gramby, you have to come downstairs now. We are about to have a family meeting, and I need you for corroboration.

You can't let them think I have lost my marbles," she said, looking at Emma. "No more family secrets about this."

"What's up with you," said Emma as Annie pulled her towards the stairs, "where's the usual crack about me and food?"

Annie spotted Josh standing at the bottom of the stairs looking up at her in confusion.

"What's all the commotion about?" he asked.

"Hey Josh, in the movie Hook, how did Peter Banning forget that he had been Peter Pan?"

"He fell in love with Wendy's daughter, stayed in London, and got a job."

"How did he get his memory back?"

"He went back to Neverland."

"Yeah," Annie smiled, "we're going back to Neverland."

It took a lot of convincing, but before the evening was over, everyone was willing to give Annie, Sophie, and Rose the benefit of the doubt about family travelers, the unknown ancestors, and the events of the day. The sketches helped, and Josh was especially affected by the pictures of Mamie and the one of him playing with the McElmurry boys.

Later that night, Annie slipped into her parents' room.

"Some day huh?" she said to her mother.

"I'll say," said Sophie.

"Mom, I'm sorry for all the times I complained about our family outings. I understand your searches better now."

Sophie laughed, "I understand my searches better now too."

Annie continued. "I need your help. I have to find the key, so I can travel again and meet other ancestors, maybe even the Unknown. And don't get mad, but I have to take Josh and Emma with me. Even if they don't remember in the present time, we'll have a blast in the past. We're a team. When they turn thirteen, they will be ready for their own travels. I'm pretty sure you're too old to go now, but you can hear about it from me and write about."

Annie laughed at the dubious expression on her mother's face.

John was listening to Sophie and Annie, satisfied that the day's events had forged a new bond between mother and daughter. He was surprised when Annie drew him into the conversation.

"Dad, I'm going to need your help too."

Pleased to be included, John puffed up and started to expound on his potential historical contributions.

"None of that stuff," said Annie. "I have a hunch the opening of the African American History and Culture Museum is going to lead to our next portal."

"I'll have to give that some thought," said John.

"Yeah, me too," smiled Annie, "me too."

Annie returned to her room, but before getting into bed, she picked up the sketchbook from the day and drew the dates on the spine.

July 2016 -July 1867.

Epilogue

My days in these sorrowful times and in this wicked place are waning. The spring and summer seasons of my life have blossomed and are now fading into fall and winter. The Architect of the Universe will soon come for the harvest.

The slaver and his overseer demand little of me now. It is not that they have the desire or the capacity to show pity; it is merely that I have so little left to give. I am stooped too low and my fingers too gnarled to be of value in the fields. If I am called upon to serve in the house, the mistress complains of my labored steps, declaring me too slow to be in her presence. I am relegated to the back kitchen, where I help cook and wash pots and plates. They consent to my existence because I am not long for this world.

I have toiled my whole life on damnable plantations, though not all of my days here have been lamentable. I have companions who stood in place of my family and loved ones. I found momentary joy in the laughter of children, in the compassionate outstretched hand that offered a cup of water on a hot day. I welcomed small comforts, laughed at the rare occasions of happiness. I wept more at outsized oppression. I mourned and rejoiced with my adopted sisters and brothers. We are living proof that the human spirit can adapt to unspeakable cruelty and still survive.

The Creator saw fit to anoint my bloodline with offspring. The slaver deprived me of the gladness to see them all to maturity. I have produced my replacements at no cost to the slavers. My children are gone, and with them, my capacity to feel. But my bitterness is fading. I neither hate nor love. I am simply tired as I prepare for the eternal rest I have earned.

I am at peace this day. I am sitting beneath an oak tree with the sun warming my face. I remember my homeland. My eye twitches involuntarily, and I don't know what to make of that. In my village, it is a sign that a visitor is coming. If another person from my village has been stolen and is brought here, I can only weep for them. If I am to be visited by a descendant, called by my spirit, then I can rejoice. At long last, they have come to hear me speak my name. I wonder who comes to visit? What message do they bring?

I hear them before I see them. They are singing the folk songs and chants of my homeland. There is joy in their chords. I see them coming down the road, beating their drums. They are wearing the ceremonial masks of my people. They have come to take me home. At long last they reach me. One steps forward and offers me her hand, and beckons me to join them. I ask if this is my life cycle ceremony? She answers, it is the life cycle ceremony for many, and it will not end for many generations. It is celebrated for each of us, and all of us through time and space, for we are Travelers and the Spirits of the Unknown Ancestors.

Author's Notes

Acknowledgments

My most profound appreciation and love go to my sister Marsha Lilienthal Boddie who has devoted the last thirty-plus years of her life and spare time researching the descendants of Fox and Mary McElmurry. She is committed to the pursuit of ensuring future generations of McElmurry and Calhoun descendants know the story of their ancestors. Marsha was the first to seek DNA testing and to discover that while we carry the genetic codes of several ethnicities, we are descended primarily from the Bamileke people of the Cameroon Region of West Africa. The Bamileke consists of over one hundred kingdoms or chiefdoms in the western province. In my effort to learn more about the Bamileke, I discovered in AFKinsider Magazine that the Bamileke people could be traced back to Egypt. They migrated to the northern part of Cameroon between the eleventh and fourteenth centuries.

Many thanks to my dear friend Martha Ritchie who knew nothing of my family or of my interest in writing a book series telling my family story. She quickly volunteered to be a sounding board. She was a tremendous help, giving the manuscript its first read and edit and she gave me the courage to proceed with a professional editor and to seek publication.

Sly as a Fox would not be possible without my mother, Alone Jones Lilienthal, who is the last surviving child of Ransom and Mamie

Calhoun Jones. She is a storyteller in her own right. Throughout my life, she has shared the tales of the trials and tribulations of growing up during the depression in the segregated South of Lizella and Macon, Georgia and the precious memories of her grandparents, Joshua Calhoun and Missouri McElmurry Calhoun.

My late aunts, Ernestine Johnson, Nellie Russell, and Odessa Sellers, and my late Uncles Earl, Rufus, and Elenzie Jones were all keepers of the dream for my cousins and me. I miss them all and hope they would be proud of my determination to tell the family story. My father, the late Walter Lilienthal, always encouraged me to seek new horizons. I see him now, with his chest pushed out, declaring this book to be the next great American novel, no matter what anyone else thinks of it.

My son, Damon, and my daughter Cydnee, along with their spouses Ivy and Damien, are an inspiration. I dedicate this book to their children. I charge you to be keepers of the flame and to pass on our story.

Finally, I thank my husband, Clarke, who has loved me, encouraged me, and been my greatest cheerleader, ensuring me that this is a worthwhile endeavor. He makes me laugh, he makes me feel safe, and he makes my life complete.

Addendum

I am aware parts of the book are heavy on history and backstory; however, the horror and offensive nature of slavery and racism are too often smoothed over in middle school and young adult literature. One cannot understand Fox and Mary, their fears, and their struggles without understanding the environment they had to survive. I am astonished at the perpetuation of a sanitized perception of the history of slavery, reconstruction, and Jim Crow. It would be a disservice to my ancestors, my children, and grandchildren to gloss over it in the telling of their family history.

Some of the book's research was challenging because of the abundant information on the American slave trade and the lives of enslaved and newly freed people. The loss of life during the Middle Passage is calculated differently by different sources. Some researchers include those who died during the "March to Confinement" before leaving the continent of Africa. Others count Africans sold into slavery to other parts of the world. Historians estimate nearly sixty million Africans were sold into slavery around the world over several hundred years.

During our summer vacations to Georgia to visit family, we attended services in Lizzie Chapel in Lizella, Georgia where I first experienced the practice of "raising a hymn." It was a powerful and genuinely moving experience and one I could not omit from this story.

The spiritual *Go Down Moses* dates to pre-Civil War and is commonly cited as a song sung by enslaved people and used by abolitionists to protest slavery. The song is based on the biblical story of Moses in the Book of Exodus, and its author is unknown. As noted in this book, spirituals were often used by enslaved people, to send and receive messages. To the unsuspecting, many of the songs of longed-for freedom were thought to refer to the afterlife. *Go Down Moses* was so direct, it was prohibited in many Southern communities where the enslaved were held. (Encyclopedia.com).

The Black Codes referenced in the chapter *Hijacked Freedom* were restrictive laws passed and imposed on African Americans after the Civil War. They were the precursors to the oppressive Jim Crow Laws that led to the Civil Rights Movement.

On occasion, my family has used the symbol of the Sankofa as a family logo. There are several versions of the legend that differ slightly, but the underlying message is the same in all of them – know where you came from to know where you are going. I am deliberately casual in the book with the frequent retelling of the legend. Fox's version is a compilation of two stories that I read.

When visiting the National Museum of African American History and Culture, my mother was deeply moved by the re-creation of a Southern cabin. In front of the cabin was a sculpture of a woman sitting in a rocking chair. The display brought my mother to tears. She said it reminded her of her grandmother. I leave it to the reader to guess the access point for Annie, Emma, and Josh's transport to the past in Missouri's Memories.

Finally, there is one document that was the inspiration for the time and location of this story. On line twenty-nine of the Georgia Returns of Qualified Voters and Reconstruction Oath Books 1867-1869, in the Third District, of Crawford County Georgia, July 23, 1867, Fox M(a)cElmurry registered to vote. He was one of two people on that page with the designation "colored."

LINKS

Middle Passage
www.digitalhistory.uh.edu/disp_textbook.cfm?smtid=2&psid=446
http://www.africanholocaust.net/news_ah/dark_voyage_hell_below.htm

Bamileke
http://www.everyculture.com/Africa-Middle-East/Bamil-k-Orientation.html#ixzz52tF5mt6f

Black Codes
https://www.history.com/topics/black-history/black-codes
https://en.wikipedia.org/wiki/Black_Codes_(United_States)
Phillis Wheatley
https://www.biography.com/people/phillis-wheatley-9528784

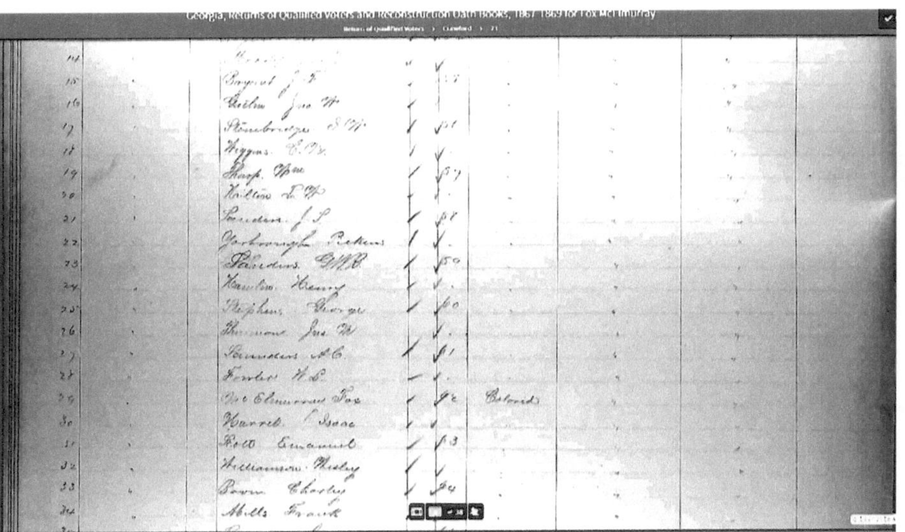

Photocopy of the voter registration page from the Crawford County Georgia Returns of Qualified Voters and Reconstruction Oath Books 1867-1869.

July 23, 1867 - Line 29 – Fox McElmurry - Colored

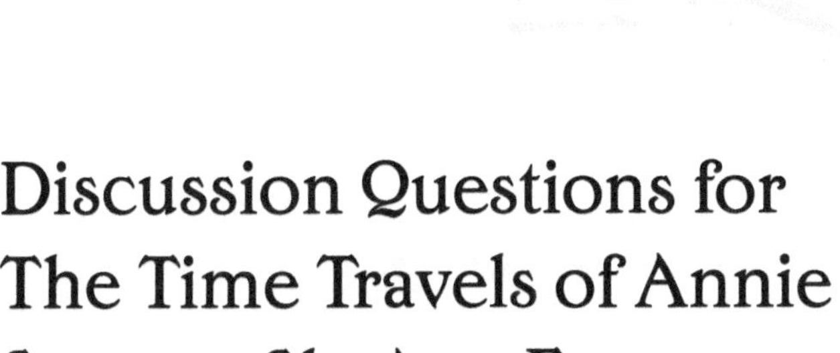

Discussion Questions for The Time Travels of Annie Sesstry: Sly As a Fox

- What was your first impression when you began reading the book?

- How did your impression change as you got into it?

- What do you think the author's purpose was in writing this book? What ideas was she trying to get across?

- What did you like best about the book?

- What did you like least?

- Who was your favorite character in the book, and why? If you picked Annie, who would be your second choice?

- Who was your least favorite character and why?

- What do you think was the purpose of the chapters of the Unknown Ancestor?

- What was your favorite quote or passage in the book?

- What feelings did the book evoke in you?

- Were there any plot points that were left unresolved or not resolved to your satisfaction?

- Did you connect with the subject matter? Did it make you want to read more? Did it make you uncomfortable?

- How did you feel about the ending? What did you like, what did you not like, and what do you wish had been different?

- Did the book make you want to read more about the time-period visited by Annie, Emma and Joshua?

- Did this book make you want to know more about your ancestors?

- When you looked at the book cover, before you read it, what did you think?

- What did you think about the cover after you read it?

- If a movie was made based on this book, who would you cast?